The Story o

Mary Hartwell Catherwood

Alpha Editions

This edition published in 2024

ISBN : 9789362995605

Design and Setting By
Alpha Editions
www.alphaedis.com
Email - info@alphaedis.com

As per information held with us this book is in Public Domain.
This book is a reproduction of an important historical work. Alpha Editions uses the best technology to reproduce historical work in the same manner it was first published to preserve its original nature. Any marks or number seen are left intentionally to preserve its true form.

Contents

INTRODUCTION. .... - 1 -

Book I. A MONTREAL BEAVER FAIR.
1678 A. D. .... - 3 -

I. FRONTENAC. .... - 5 -

II HAND-OF-IRON. .... - 9 -

III. FATHER HENNEPIN. .... - 13 -

IV. A COUNCIL. .... - 18 -

V. SAINTE JEANNE. .... - 22 -

VI. THE PROPHECY OF JOLYCŒUR. .... - 27 -

Book II. FORT FRONTENAC. 1683 A. D. .... - 33 -

I. RIVAL MASTERS. .... - 35 -

II. A TRAVELLED FRIAR. .... - 40 -

III. HEAVEN AND EARTH. .... - 42 -

IV. A CANOE FROM THE ILLINOIS. .... - 47 -

V. FATHER HENNEPIN'S CHAPEL. .... - 53 -

VI. LA SALLE AND TONTY. .... - 57 -

VII. AN ADOPTION. .... - 61 -

VIII. TEGAHKOUITA. .... - 65 -

IX. AN ORDEAL. .... - 69 -

X. HEMLOCK. .... - 73 -

Book III. FORT ST. LOUIS OF THE
ILLINOIS. 1687 A. D. .... - 77 -

I. IN AN EAGLE'S NEST .... - 79 -

II. THE FRIEND AND BROTHER .... - 83 -

III. HALF-SILENCE. .... - 88 -

IV. A FÊTE ON THE ROCK. .... - 93 -

V. THE UNDESPAIRING NORMAN .... - 98 -

VI. TO-DAY. .... - 104 -

FOOTNOTES: .... - 106 -

INTRODUCTION.

No man can see all of a mountain at once. He sees its differing sides. Moreover, it has rainy and bright day aspects, and summer and winter faces.

The romancer is covered with the dust of old books, modern books, great books, and out of them all brings in a condensing hand these pictures of two men whose lives were as large as this continent.

La Salle is a definite figure in the popular mind. But La Salle's greater friend is known only to historians and students. To me the finest fact in the Norman explorer's career is the devotion he commanded in Henri de Tonty. No stupid dreamer, no ruffian at heart, no betrayer of friendship, no mere blundering woodsman—as La Salle has been outlined by his enemies—could have bound to himself a man like Tonty. The love of this friend and the words this friend has left on record thus honor La Salle. And we who like courage and steadfastness and gentle courtesy in men owe much honor which has never been paid to Henri de Tonty.

BOOK I.
A MONTREAL BEAVER FAIR.
1678 A. D.

I.
FRONTENAC.

Along the entire river front of Montreal camp-fires faded as the amphitheatre of night gradually dissolved around them.

Canoes lay beached in one long row as if a shoal of huge fish had come to land. The lodges made a new street along Montreal wharf. Oblong figures of Indian women moved from shadow to shine, and children stole out to caper beside kettles where they could see their breakfasts steaming. Here and there light fell upon a tranquil mummy less than a metre in length, standing propped against a lodge side, and blinking stoical eyes in its brown flat face as only a bark-encased Indian baby could blink; or it slept undisturbed by the noise of the awakening camp, looking a mummy indeed.

The savage of the New World carried his family with him on every peaceable journey; sometimes to starve for weeks when the winter hunting proved bad. It was only when he went to war that he denied himself all squaw service.

The annual beaver fair was usually held in midsummer, but this year the tribes of the upper lakes had not descended with their furs to Montreal until September. These precious skins, taken out of the canoes, were stored within the lodges.

Every male of the camp was already greasing, painting, and feathering himself for the grand council, which always preceded a beaver fair. Hurons, Ottawas, Crees, Nipissings, Ojibwas, Pottawatamies, each jealous for his tribe, completed a process begun the night before, and put on what might be called his court dress. In some cases this was no dress at all, except a suit of tattooing, or a fine coat of ochre streaked with white clay or soot. The juice of berries heightened nature in their faces. But there were grand barbarians who laid out robes of beaver skin, ample, and marked inside with strange figures or porcupine quill embroidery. The heads swarming in this vast and dusky dressing-room were some of them shaven bare except the scalp lock, some bristling in a ridge across the top, while others carried the natural coarse growth tightly braided down one side, with the opposite half flowing loose.

Montreal behind its palisades made a dim background to all this early illumination,—few domestic candles shining through windows or glancing about the Hôtel Dieu as the nuns began their morning devotions. Mount Royal now flickered a high shadow, and now massed inertly against stars;

but the river, breathing forever like some colossal creature, reflected all the camp-fires in its moving scales.

The guns of the fort had fired a salute to Indian guests on their arrival the evening before. But at sunrise repeated cannonading, a prolonged roll of drums, and rounds of musketry announced that the governor-general's fleet was in sight.

Montreal flocked to the wharf where already the savages were arrayed in solemn ranks. Marching out of the fortress with martial music, past the Hôtel Dieu to the landing-place where Frontenac must step from his boat, came the remnant of the Carignan regiment. Even the Sulpitian brotherhood, whose rights as seigniors of Montreal island this governor had at one time slighted, appeared to do him honor. And gentle nuns of St. Joseph were seen in the general outpour of inhabitants.

This governor-general, with all his faults, had a large and manly way of meeting colonial dangers, and was always a prop under the fainting heart of New France.

His boats made that display upon the St. Lawrence which it was his policy and inclination to make before Indians. Officers in white and gold, and young nobles of France, powdered, and flashing in the colors of Louis' magnificent reign, crowded his own vessel,—young men who had ventured out to Quebec because it was the fashion at court to be skilled in colonial matters, and now followed Frontenac as far as Montreal to amuse themselves with the annual beaver fair. The flag of France, set with its lily-like symbol, waved over their heads its white reply to its twin signal on the fort.

Frontenac stood at the boat's prow, his rich cloak thrown back, and his head bared to the morning river breath and the people's shouts. Being colonial king pleased this soldier, tired of European camps and the full blaze of royalty, where his poverty put him to the disadvantage of a singed moth.

He came blandly gliding to the wharf, Louis de Buade, Count of Frontenac, and Baron of Palluau, and the only governor of New France who ever handled the arrogant Five Nations of the Iroquois like a strong father,[1]—a man who would champion the rights of his meanest colonist, and at the same time quarrel with his lieutenant in power to his last breath.

Merchants of Quebec followed him with boat-loads of Indian supplies. Even Acadia had sent men to this voyage, for the Baron de Saint-Castin appeared in the fleet, with his young Indian Baroness. It is told of Saint-Castin that he had kept a harem in his sylvan principality of Pentegoet; but being a man of conscience, he confessed and reformed. It is also told of him that he never kept a harem or otherwise lapsed into the barbarisms of the Penobscots, among whom he carried missionaries and over whom he was a great lord. Type of the Frenchman of his day, he came to New France a lad in the Carignan regiment, amassed fortunes in the fur trade, and holding his own important place in the colony, goaded like a thorn the rival colony of New England along his borders.

But most conspicuous to the eyes of Montreal were two men standing at Frontenac's right hand, a Norman and an Italian. Both were tall, the Italian being of deeper colors and more generous materials. His large features were clothed in warm brown skin. Rings of black hair thick as a fleece were cut short above his military collar. His fearless, kindly eyes received impressions from every aspect of the New World. There dwelt in Henri de Tonty the power to make men love him at sight,—savages as well as Europeans. He wore the dress of a French lieutenant of infantry, and looked less than thirty years old, having entered the service of France in his early youth.

The other man, Robert Cavelier,—called La Salle from an estate he had once owned in France,—explorer, and seignior of Fort Frontenac and adjacent grants on the north shore of Lake Ontario, was at that time in the prime of his power. He was returning from France, with the king's permission to work out all his gigantic enterprises, with funds for the purpose, and one of the most promising young military men in Europe as his lieutenant.

Montreal merchants on the wharf singled out La Salle with jealous eye, which saw in the drooping point and flaring base of his nose an endless smile of scorn. He was a man who had only to use his monopolies to become enormously rich, cutting off the trade of the lakes from Montreal. That he was above gain, except as he could use it for hewing his ambitious road into the wilderness, they did not believe. The merchants of Montreal readily translated the shyness and self-restraint of his solitary nature into the arrogance of a recently ennobled and successful man.

La Salle had a spare face, with long oval cheeks, curving well inward beside the round of his sensitive prominent chin. Gray and olive tones still further cooled the natural pallor of his skin and made ashen brown the hair which he wore flowing.

The plainness of an explorer and the elegance of a man exact in all his habits distinguished La Salle's dress against that background of brilliant courtiers.

He moved ashore with Frontenac, who saluted benignly both the array of red allies and the inhabitants of this second town in the province.

The sub-governor stepped out to escort the governor-general to the fort, bells rang, cannon still boomed, martial music pierced the heart with its thrill, and the Carignan squad wheeled in behind Frontenac's moving train.

"Sieur de la Salle! Sieur de la Salle!" a little girl called, breaking away from the Sisters of St. Joseph, whose convent robes had enclosed her like palisades, "take me also in the procession!"

This demand granted itself, so nimbly did she escape a nun's ineffectual grasp and spring between Tonty and La Salle.

Frontenac himself had turned at the shrill outcry. He laughed when he saw the wilful young creature taking the explorer by the wrist and falling into step so close to his own person.

A pursuing nun, unwilling to interrupt the governors train, hovered along its progress, making anxious signs to her charge, until she received an assuring gesture from La Salle. She then went back dissatisfied but relieved of responsibility; and the child, with a proud fling of her person, marched on toward the fort.

II
HAND-OF-IRON.

"Mademoiselle the tiger-cat," said La Salle to Tonty, making himself heard with some effort above the din of martial sound.

The young soldier lifted his hat with his left hand and made the child a bow, which she regarded with critical eyes.

"I am the niece of Monsieur de la Salle," she explained to Tonty as she marched; "so he calls me tiger-cat."

"Mademoiselle Barbe Cavelier is the tiger-cat's human name," the explorer added, laughing. "It is flattering to have this nimble animal spring affectionately on one from ambush; but I should soon have inquired after you at the convent, mademoiselle."

"I did not spring affectionately on you," said Barbe; "I wanted to be in the procession."

"Hast thou then lost all regard for thy uncle La Salle during his year of absence?"

Barbe's high childish voice distinctly and sincerely stated, "No, monsieur; I have fought all the girls at the convent on your account. Jeanne le Ber said nothing against you; but she is a Le Ber. I am glad you came back in such grandeur. I was determined to be in the grandeur myself. But it is not a time to give you my cheek for a kiss."

La Salle smiled over her head at Tonty. The Italian noted her marked resemblance to the explorer. She had the same features in delicate tints, the darkness of her eyelashes and curls only emphasizing the type. Already her small nose drooped at the point and flared at the base. As La Salle and his young kinswoman stepped together, Tonty gauged them alike,—two self-restraining natures with unmeasured endurance and individual force like the electric current.

Montreal's square bastioned fort, by the mouth of a small creek flowing into the St. Lawrence, was soon reached from the wharf. It stood at the south end of the town.

"My dear child," said La Salle, stating his case to Barbe, "it is necessary for me to go into the fort with Count Frontenac, and equally necessary you should go back at once to the Sisters. I will bring you out of the convent to-morrow to look at the beaver fair. This is Monsieur de Tonty, my lieutenant; let him take you back to the nuns. I shall be blamed if I carry you into the fort."

Barbe heard him without raising objections. She looked at Tonty, who gave her his left hand and drew her out of the train.

It swept past them into the fortress gates,—gallant music, faces returning her eager gaze with smiles, plumes, powdered curls, and laces, gold and white uniforms, soldiers with the sun flashing from their gun-barrels.

Barbe watched the last man in. To express her satisfaction she then rose to the tip of one foot and hopped three steps. She was lightly and delicately made, and as full of restless grace as a bird. Her face and curls bloomed above and strongly contrasted with the raiment her convent guardians planned for a child dependent, not on their charity, but on their maternal care.

The September morning enveloped the world in a haze of brightness, like that perfecting blue breath which we call the bloom upon the grape. A great landscape with a scarf of melting azure resting around its horizon, or ravelling to shreds against the mountain's breast, or pretending to be wood-smoke across the river, drew Tonty's eye from the disappearing pageant.

That fair land was a fit spot whereon the most luxurious of civilizations should touch and affiliate with savages of the wilderness. Up the limpid green river the Lachine Rapids showed their teeth with audible roar. From that point Mount Royal could be seen rising out of mists and stretching its hind-quarters westward like some vast mastodon. But to Tonty only its front appeared, a globe dipped in autumn colors and wearing plumes of vapor. The sky of this new hemisphere rose in unmeasured heights which the eye followed in vain; there seemed no zenith to the swimming blinding azure.

A row of booths for merchants had been built all along the outside of Montreal's palisades, and traders were thus early setting their goods in array.

At the north extremity of the town that huge stone windmill built by the seigniors for defence, cast a long dewy shadow toward the west. Its loopholes showed like dark specks on the body of masonry.

Sun-sparkles on the river were no more buoyant and changeable than the child at Tonty's side. Dimples came and went in her cheeks. Her blood was stirred by the swarming life around her.

"Monsieur," she confided to her uncle's lieutenant, "I am meditating something very wicked."

"Certainly that is impossible, mademoiselle," said Tonty, accommodating his step to her reluctant gait.

"I am meditating on not going back to the convent."

"Where would you go, mademoiselle?"

"Everywhere, to see things."

"But my orders are to escort you to the nuns. You would disgrace me as a soldier."

Barbe lifted her gaze to his face and was diverted from rebellion. Tonty put out his arm to guard her, but a tall stalking brave was pushed against her in passing and immediately startled by the thud of her prompt fist upon his back. The Indian turned, unsheathing his knife.

"Get out of my way, thou ugly big warrior," said Barbe, meeting his eye, which softened from fierceness to laughter, and holding her fist ready for further encounter.

The Indian made some mocking gestures and menaced her playfully with his thumb. Tonty threw his arm across her shoulder and moved her on toward the convent. Barbe escaped from this touch, an entirely new matter filling her mind.

"Monsieur, even old Jonaneaux in our Hôtel Dieu hath not such a heavy hand as thou hast. Many a time hath he pulled me down off the palisade when I looked over to see the coureurs de bois go roaring by. But thou hast a hand like iron!"

Tonty flushed, being not yet hardened to his misfortune.

"It is a hand of iron. I am called Main-de-fer."[2]

Barbe took hold of it in its glove. Of all the people she had ever met Tonty was the only person whose touch she did not resent.

"The other hand is not like unto it, monsieur?"

He gave her the other also, and she compared their weight. With a roguish lifting of her nostrils she inquired,—

"Will every bit of you turn to metal like this heavy hand?"

"Alas, no, mademoiselle; there is no hope of that."

Tonty stripped his gauntlet off. With half afraid fingers she examined the artificial member. It was of copper.

"Where is the old one, monsieur?"

"It was blown off by a grenade at Messina last year."

"Does it hurt?"

"Not now. Except when I think of the service of Monsieur de la Salle, and of my being thus pieced out as a man."

Barbe measured his height and breadth and warm-toned face with satisfied eyes. She consoled him.

"There is so much of you, monsieur, you can easily do without a hand."

III.
FATHER HENNEPIN.

"Thou art a comfort to a soldier, mademoiselle," said Tonty, heartily.

"But not to a priest," observed Barbe. "For last birthday when I was eleven my uncle Abbé stuck out his lip and said I was eleven years bad. But my uncle La Salle kissed my cheek. There goeth François le Moyne." Her face became suddenly distorted with grimaces of derision beside which Tonty could scarcely keep his gravity. A boy of about her own age ran past, dropping her a sneer for her pains.

"Monsieur, these Le Moynes and Sorels and Bouchers and Varennes and Joliets and Le Bers, they are all against my uncle La Salle. The girls talk about it in the convent. But he hath the governor on his side, so what can they do? I have pinched Jeanne le Ber at school, but she will never pinch back and it only makes her feel holier. So I pinch her no more. Do you know Jeanne le Ber?"

"No," said Tonty, "I have not that pleasure."

"Oh, monsieur, it is no pleasure. She says so many prayers. When I have prayers for penances they make me so tired I have to get up and hop between them. But Jeanne le Ber would pray all the time if her father did not pull her off her knees. My father and mother died in France. If they were alive they would not have to pull me off my knees."

"But a woman should learn to pray, even as a man should learn to fight," observed Tonty. "He stands between her and danger, and she should stand linking him to heaven."

"I can fight for myself," said Barbe. "And everybody ought to say his own prayers; but it makes one disagreeable to say more than his share. I wish to grow up an agreeable person."

They had reached the palisade entrance which fronted the river, Barbe's feet still lagging amid the lively scenes outside. She allowed Tonty to lead her with his left hand, thus sheltering her next the booths from streams of passing Indians and traders.

Beside this open gate she would have lingered indefinitely, chattering to a guardian who felt her hatred of convent restraint, and gazing at preparations for the council: at prunes and chopped pieces of oxen being put to boil for an Indian feast; at the governor's chair from the fortress, where the sub-governor lived, borne by men to the middle of that space yearly occupied as the council ring. But a watchful Sister was hovering ready inside the palisade gate, and reaching forth her arm she drew her charge away from Tonty, giving him brief and scandalized thanks for his service.

Barbe looked back. It was worth Tonty's while to catch sight of that regretful face smeared about its warm neck by curls, its lips parted to repeat and still repeat, "Adieu, monsieur. Adieu, monsieur."

But two men had come between the disappearing child and him, one man, dressed partly like an officer and partly like a coureur de bois, throwing both arms around Tonty in the eager Latin manner.

"My cousin Henri de Tonty, welcome to the New World. I waited with my gouty leg at the fortress for you; but when you came not, like a good woodsman, I tracked you down."

"My cousin Greysolon du Lhut! Glad am I to find you so speedily. This cold and heavy hand belies me."

"I heard of this hand. But the other was well lost, my cousin. Take courage in beholding me; I had nearly lost a leg, and not by good powder and shot either, but with gout which disgracefully loads up a man with his own dead members. But the Iroquois virgin, Catharine Tegahkouita, hath interceded for me."

"Monsieur de Tonty will observe we have saints among the savages in New France," said the other man.

He was a Récollet friar with sandalled feet, wearing a gray capote of coarse texture which was girt with the cord of Saint Francis. His peaked hood hung behind his shoulders leaving his shaven crown to glisten with rosy enjoyment of the sunlight. A crucifix hung at his side; but no man ever devoted his life to prayer who was so manifestly created to enjoy the world. He had a nose of Flemish amplitude depressed in the centre, fat lips, a terraced chin, and twinkling good-humored eyes. The gray capote could not conceal a pompous swell of the stomach and the strut of his sandalled feet.

"My cousin Tonty," said Du Lhut, "this is Father Louis Hennepin from Fort Frontenac. He hath come down to Montreal[3] to meet Monsieur de la Salle and engage himself in the new western venture."

"Venture!" exclaimed a keen-visaged man in the garb of a merchant-colonist who was carrying a bale of goods to one of the booths,—for no man in Montreal was ashamed to get profit out of the beaver fair. "Where your Monsieur de la Salle is concerned there will be venture enough, but no results for any man but La Salle."

He set his bale down as if it were a challenge.

Points of light sprung into Tonty's eyes and the blood in his face showed its quickening.

"Monsieur," he spoke, "if you are a gentleman you shall answer to me for slandering Monsieur de la Salle."

"Monsieur," spoke Tonty, "if you are a gentleman you shall answer to me for slandering Monsieur de la Salle."—*Page 32.*

"Jacques le Ber is a noble of the colony," declared Du Lhut, with the derisive freedom this great ranger and leader of coureurs de bois assumed toward any one; "for hath he not purchased his patent of King Louis for six thousand livres? But look you, my cousin Tonty, if the king allowed not us colonial nobles to engage in trade he would lose us all by starvation; for scarce a miserable censitaire on our lands can pay us his capon and pint of wheat at the end of the year."

"I will answer to you, monsieur," said Jacques le Ber to the soldier, "that La Salle is the enemy of the colony, and the betrayer of them that have been his friends."

Father Hennepin and Du Lhut caught Tonty's arms. Du Lhut then dragged him with expostulations inside the palisade gate, repeating Frontenac's strict orders that all quarrels should be suppressed during the beaver fair, and as the young man's furious looks still sought the merchant, reminding him of the harm he might do La Salle by an open quarrel with Montreal traders.

"I, who am not bound to La Salle as close as thou art,—I tell you it will not do," declared Du Lhut.

"Let the man keep his distance, then!"

"Why, you hot-blooded fellow! why do you take these Frenchmen so seriously?"

"Sieur de la Salle is my friend. I will strike any man who denounces him."

"Oh, come out toward the mountain. Let us make a little pilgrimage," laughed Du Lhut. "We must cool thee, Tonty, we must cool thee; or La Salle's enemies will lie in one heap the length of Montreal, mowed by this iron hand!"

As Jacques le Ber carried forward his bale, Father Hennepin walked beside him dealing forth good-natured remonstrance with fat hands and out-turned lips.

"My son, God save me from the man who doth nurse a grievance. Your case is simply this: our governor built a fort at Cataraqui, and it is now called Fort Frontenac. He put you and associates of yours in charge, and you had profit of that fort. Afterward, by his recommendation to the king, Sieur de la Salle was made seignior of Fort Frontenac and lands thereabout. This hast thou ever since bitterly chewed to the poisoning of thy immortal soul."

"You churchmen all,—Jesuits, Sulpitians, or Récollets,—are over zealous to domineer in this colony," spoke Jacques le Ber, through the effort of carrying his bale.

"My son," said Father Hennepin, swelling his stomach and inflating his throat, "why should I enter the mendicant order of Saint Francis and live according to the rules of a pure and severe virtue, if I felt no zeal for saving souls?"

"I spoke of domineering," repeated the angry merchant.

"And touching Monsieur de la Salle," said Father Hennepin, "I exhort thee not to love him; for who could love him,—but to rid thyself of hatred of any one."

"Father Hennepin has not then attached himself to La Salle's new enterprise?"

"I have a grand plan of discovery of my own," said the friar, deeply, rolling his shaven head, "an enterprise which would terrify anybody but me. The Sieur de la Salle merely opens my path. I will confess to thee, my son, that in youth I often hid myself behind the doors of taverns,—which were no fit haunts for men of holy life,—to hearken unto sailors' tales of strange lands. And thus would I willingly do without eating or drinking, such burning desire I had to explore new countries."

The Father did not observe that Jacques le Ber had reached his own booth and was there arranging his goods regardless of explorations in strange lands, but walked on, talking to the air, his out-thrust lips rounding every word, until some derisive savage pointed out this solo.

Jacques le Ber made ready to take his place in the governor's council, thinking wrathfully of his encounter with Tonty. He dwelt, as we all do, upon the affronts and hindrances of the present, rather than on his prospect of founding a strong and worthy family in the colony.

IV.
A COUNCIL.

The North American savage, with an unerring instinct which republics might well study, sent his wisest men to the front to represent him.

A great circle of Indians, ranged according to their tribes, sat around Frontenac when the stone windmill trod its noon shadow underfoot. Te Deum had been sung in the chapel, and thanks offered for his safe arrival. The principal men of Montreal, with the governor's white and gold officers, sat now within the circle behind his chair.

But Frontenac faced every individual of his Indian children, moving before them, their natural leader, as he made his address of greeting, admonition, and approval, through Du Lhut as interpreter. The old courtier loved Indians. They appealed to that same element in him which the coureurs de bois knew how to reach. The Frenchman has a wild strain of blood. He takes kindly and easily to the woods. He makes himself an appropriate and even graceful figure against any wilderness background, and goes straight to Nature's heart, carrying all the refinements of civilization with him.

The smoke of the peace pipe went up hour after hour. By strictest rules of precedence each red orator rose in his turn and spoke his tribe's reply to Onontio.[4] An Indian never hurried eloquence. The sun might tip toward Mount Royal, and the steam of his own deferred feast reach his nose in delicious suggestion. He had to raise the breeze of prosperity, to clear the sun, to wipe away tears for friends slain during past misunderstandings with Onontio's other children, and to open the path of peace between their lodges and the lodges of his tribe. Ottawa, Huron, Cree, Nipissing, Ojibwa, or Pottawatamie, it was necessary for him to bury the hatchet in pantomime, to build a great council-fire whose smoke should rise to heaven in view of all the nations, and gather the tribes of the lakes in one family council with the French around this fire forever.

"**Each red orator rose in his turn and spoke his tribe's reply.**"—*Page 40.*

Children played along the river's brink, and squaws kept fire under the kettles. A few men guarded the booths along the palisades from pilferers, though scarce a possible pilferer roamed from the centre of interest.

Crowds of spectators pressed around the great circle; traders who had brought packs of skins skilfully intercepted by them at some station above Montreal; interpreters, hired by merchants to serve them during the fair; coureurs de bois stretching up their neck sinews until these knotted with intense and prolonged effort. In this standing wall the habitant was crowded by converted Iroquois from the Mountain mission, who, having learned their rights as Christians, yielded no inch of room.

The sun descended out of sight behind Mount Royal, though his presence lingered with sky and river in abundant crimsons. Still the smoke of the peace pipe rose above the council ring, and eloquence rolled its periods on. That misty scarf around the horizon, which high noon drove out of sight, floated into view again, becoming denser and denser. The pipings of outdoor insects came sharpened through twilight, and all the camp-fires were deepening their hue, before a solemn uprising of Frenchmen and Indians proclaimed the council over.

La Salle had sat through it at the governor's right hand, watching those bronze faces and restless eyes with sympathy as great as Frontenac's. He, also, was a lord of the wilderness. He could more easily open his shy nature to such red brethren and eloquently command, denounce, or persuade them, than stand before dames and speak one word,—which he was forced to attempt when candles were lighted in the candelabra of the fort.

There was not such pageantry at Montreal as in the more courtly society of Quebec. The appearance of the governor with his train of young nobles drew out those gentler inhabitants who took no part in the bartering of the beaver fair.

Perrot, the sub-governor, had known his period of bitter disagreement with Frontenac. Having made peace with a superior he once defied, he was anxious to pay Frontenac every honor, and the two governors were united in their policy of amusing and keeping busy so varied an assemblage as that which thronged the beaver fair. Festivity as grand as colonial circumstances permitted was therefore held in the governor's apartments. The guarded fortress gates stood open; torches burned within the walls, and blanketed savages stalked in and out.

Yet that colonial drawing-room lacked the rude elements which go to making most pioneer societies. Human intercourse in frontier towns exposed to danger and hardship, though it may be hearty and innocent, is rarely graceful.

But here was a small Versailles transplanted to the wilderness. Fragments of a great court met Indian-wedded nobles and women with generations of good ancestors behind them. Here were even the fashions of the times in gowns, and the youths of Louis' salon bowed and paid compliments to powdered locks. These French colonial nobles were poor; but with pioneer instinct they decorated themselves with the best garments their scanty money would buy. Here thronged Dumays, Le Moynes, Mousniers, Desroches, Fleurys, Baudrys, Migeons, Vigers, Gautiers, all chattering and animated. Here stood the Baroness de Saint-Castin like a statue of bronze. Here were those illustrious Le Moynes, father and sons, whose deeds may be traced in our day from the St. Lawrence to the Gulf of Mexico. Here Frontenac, with the graciously winning manner which belonged to his pleasant hours, drew to himself and soothed disaffected magnates of his colonial kingdom.

All these figures, and the spectacles swarming around the beaver fair, like combinations in a kaleidoscope to be seen once and seen no more, gave Tonty such condensed knowledge of the New World as no ordinary days could offer.

La Salle alone, though fresh from audiences at court and distinguished by royal favor, stood abashed and annoyed by the part he must play toward civilized people.

"Look at the Sieur de la Salle," observed Du Lhut to Tonty. "There is a man who stands and fights off the approach of every other creature."

"There never was a man better formed for friendship," retorted Tonty. "Touching his reserve, I call that no blemish, though he has said of it himself, it is a defect he can never be rid of as long as he lives, and often it spites him against himself."

La Salle turned his shoulder on these associates, uneasily conscious that his weakness was observed, and put many moving figures between himself and them. He had the free gait of a woodsman tempered by the air of a courtier. More than one Montreal girl accusing gold-embroidered young soldiers of finding the Quebec women charming, turned her eyes to follow La Salle. Possible lord of the vast and unknown west, in the flower of his years, he was next to Frontenac the most considerable figure in the colony.

Severe study in early youth and ambition in early manhood had crowded the lover out of La Salle. His practical gaze was oppressed by so many dames. It dwelt upon the floor, until, travelling accidentally to a corner, it rose and encountered Jacques le Ber's daughter sitting beside her mother.

V.
SAINTE JEANNE.

When La Salle was seignior of Lachine, before the king and Frontenac helped his ambition to its present foothold, he had been in the habit of stopping at Jacques le Ber's house when he came to Montreal.

The first day of the beaver fair greatly tasked Madame le Ber. She sat drowsily beside the eldest child of her large absent flock, and was not displeased to have her husband's distinguished enemy approach Jeanne.

The wife of Le Ber had been called madame since her husband bought his patent of nobility; but she held no strict right to the title, even wives of the lesser nobles being then addressed as demoiselles. In that simple colonial life Jacques le Ber, or his wife in his absence, served goods to customers over his own counter. Madame le Ber was an excellent woman, who said her prayers and approached the sacraments at proper seasons. She had abundant flesh covered with dark red skin, and she often pondered why a spirit of a daughter with passionate longings after heaven had been sent to her. If Sieur de la Salle could draw the child's mind from extreme devotion, her husband must feel indebted to him.

La Salle's face relaxed and softened as he sat down beside this sixteen-year-old maid in her colonial gown. She held her crucifix in her hands, and waited for him to talk. Jeanne made melody of his silences. As a child she had never rubbed against him for caresses, but looked into his eyes with sincere meditation. Having no idea of the explorer's aim, Jeanne le Ber was yet in harmony with him across their separating years. She also could stake her life on one supreme idea. La Salle was formed to subdue the wilderness; she was dimly and ignorantly, but with her childish might, undertaking that stranger region, the human soul. She looked younger than other girls of her age; yet La Salle was moved to say, using the name he had given her,—

"You have changed much since last year, Sainte Jeanne."

"Am I worse, Sieur de la Salle?" she anxiously inquired.

"No. Better. Except I fear you have prayed yourself to a greater distance from me."

"I name you in my prayers, Sieur de la Salle. Ever since my father ceased to be your friend I have asked to have your haughty spirit humbled."

La Salle laughed.

"If you name me at all, Sainte Jeanne, pray rather for the humbling of my enemies."

"No, Sieur de la Salle. You need your enemies. I could ill do without mine."

"Who could be an enemy to thee?"

"There are many enemies of my soul. One is my great, my very great love."

La Salle's face whitened and flushed. He cast a quick glance upon the dozing matron, the backs of people whose conversation buzzed about his ears, and returned to Jeanne's childlike white eyelids and crucifix-folding hands.

"Whom do you love, Sainte Jeanne?"

"I love my father so much, and my mother; and the children are too dear to me. Sometimes when I rise in the night to pray, and think of living apart from my dear father, the cold sweat stands on my forehead. Too many dear people throng between the soul and heaven. Even you, Sieur de la Salle,—I have to pray against thoughts of you."

"Do not pray against me, Sainte Jeanne," said the explorer, with a wistful tremor of the lower lip. "Consider how few there be that love me well."

Her eyes rested on him with divining gaze. Jeanne le Ber's eyes had the singular function of sending innumerable points of light swimming through the iris, as if the soul were in motion and shaking off sparkles.

"If you lack love and suffer thereby," she instructed him, "it will profit your soul."

La Salle interlaced his fingers, resting his hands upon his knees, and gave her a look which was both amused and tender.

"And what other enemies has Sainte Jeanne?"

"Sieur de la Salle, have I not often told you what a sinner I am? It ridicules me to call me saint."

"Since you have grown to be a young demoiselle I ought to call you Mademoiselle le Ber."

"Call me Sainte Jeanne rather than that. I do not want to be a young demoiselle, or in this glittering company. It is my father who insists."

"Nor do I want to be in this glittering company, Sainte Jeanne."

"The worst of all the other enemies, Sieur de la Salle, are vanity and a dread of enduring pain. I am very fond of dress." The young creature drew a deep regretful breath.

"But you mortify this fondness?" said La Salle, accompanying with whimsical sympathy every confession of Jeanne le Ber's.

"Indeed I have to humiliate myself often—often. When this evil desire takes strong hold, I put on the meanest rag I can find. But my father and mother will never let me go thus humbled to Mass."

"Therein do I commend your father and mother," said La Salle; "though the outside we bear toward men is of little account. But tell me how do you school yourself to pain, Sainte Jeanne? I have not learned to bear pain well in all my years."

Jeanne again met his face with swarming lights in her eyes. Seeing that no one observed them she bent her head toward La Salle and parted the hair over her crown. The straight fine growth was very thick and of a brown color. It reminded him of midwinter swamp grasses springing out of a bed of snow. A mat of burrs was pressed to this white scalp. Some of the hair roots showed red stains.

"These hurt me all the time," said Jeanne. "And it is excellent torture to comb them out."

She covered the burrs with a swift pressure, tightly closing her mouth and eyes with the spasm of pain this caused, and once more took and folded the crucifix within her hands.

The explorer made no remonstrance against such self-torture, though his practical gaze remained on her youthful brier-crowned head. He heard a girl in front of him laugh to a courtier who was flattering her.

"Hé, monsieur, I have myself seen Quebec women who dressed with odious taste."

But Jeanne, wrapped in her own relation, continued with a tone which slighted mere physical pain,—

"There is a better way to suffer, Sieur de la Salle, and that is from ill-treatment. Such anguish can be dealt out by the hands we love; but I have no friend willing to discipline me thus. My father's servant Jolycœur is the only person who makes me as wretched as I ought to be."

"Discipline through Jolycœur," said La Salle, laughing, "is what my proud stomach could never endure."

"Perhaps you have not such need, Sieur de la Salle. My father has many times turned him off, but I plead until he is brought back. He hath this whole year been a means of grace to me by his great impudence. If I say to him, 'Jolycœur, do this or that,' he never fails to reply, 'Do it yourself, Mademoiselle Jeanne,' and adds profanity to make Heaven blush. Whenever he can approach near enough, he whispers contemptuous names at me, so that I cannot keep back the tears. Yet how little I endure, when Saint Lawrence perished on a gridiron, and all the other holy martyrs shame me!"

"Your father does not suffer these things to be done to you?"

"No, Sieur de la Salle. My father knows naught of it except my pity. He did once kick Jolycœur, who left our house three days, so that I was in danger of sinking in slothful comfort. But I got him brought back, and he lay drunk in our garden with his mouth open, so that my soul shuddered to look at him. It was excellent discipline,"[5] said Jeanne, with a long breath.

"Jolycœur will better adorn the woods and risk his worthless neck on water for my uses, than longer chafe your tender nature," said La Salle. "He has been in my service before, and craved to-day that I would enlist him again."

"Had my father turned him off?" asked Jeanne, with consternation.

"He said Jacques le Ber had lifted a hand against him for innocently neglecting to carry bales of merchandise to a booth."

"I did miss the smell of rum downstairs before we came away," said the girl, sadly. "And will you take my scourge from me, Sieur de la Salle?"

"I will give him a turn at suffering himself," answered La Salle. "The fellow shall be whipped on some pretext when I get him within Fort Frontenac, for every pang he hath laid upon you. He is no stupid. He knew what he was doing."

"Oh, Sieur de la Salle, Jolycœur was only the instrument of Heaven. He is not to blame."

"If I punish him not, it will be on your promise to seek no more torments, Sainte Jeanne."

"There are no more for me to seek; for who in our house will now be unkind to me? But, Sieur de la Salle, I feel sure that during my lifetime I shall be permitted to suffer as much as Heaven could require."

Man and child, each surrounded by his peculiar world, sat awhile longer together in silence, and then La Salle joined the governor.

VI.
THE PROPHECY OF JOLYCŒUR.

By next mid-day the beaver fair was at its height, and humming above the monotone of the St. Lawrence.

Montreal, founded by religious enthusiasts and having the Sulpitian priests for its seigniors, was a quiet town when left to itself,—when the factions of Quebec did not meet its own factions in the street with clubs; or coureurs de bois roar along the house sides in drunken joy; or sudden glares on the night landscape with attendant screeching proclaim an Iroquois raid; or this annual dissipation in beaver skins crowd it for two days with strangers.

Among colonists who had thronged out to meet the bearers of colonial riches as soon as the first Indian canoe was beached, were the coureurs de bois. They still swarmed about, making or renewing acquaintances, here acting as interpreters and there trading on their own account.

Before some booths Indians pressed in rows, demanding as much as the English gave for their furs, though the price was set by law. French merchants poked their fingers into the satin pliancy of skins to search for flaws. Dealers who had no booths pressed with their interpreters from tribe to tribe,—small merchants picking the crumbs of profit from under their brethren's tables. There was greedy demand for the first quality of skins; for beaver came to market in three grades: "Castor gras, castor demi-gras, et castor sec."

The booths were hung with finery, upon which squaws stood gazing with a stoical eye to be envied by civilized woman.

The cassocks of Sulpitians and gray capotes of Récollet Fathers—favorites of Frontenac who hated Jesuits—penetrated in constant supervision every recess of the beaver fair. Yet in spite of this religious care rum was sold, its effects increasing as the day moved on.

A hazy rosy atmosphere had shorn the sun so that he hung a large red globe in the sky. The land basked in melting tints. Scarcely any wind flowed on the river. Ste. Helen's Island and even Mount Royal, the seminary and stone windmill, the row of wooden houses and palisade tips, all had their edges blurred by hazy light.

Amusement could hardly be lacking in any gathering of French people not assembled for ceremonies of religion. In Quebec the governor's court were inclined to entertain themselves with their own performance of spectacles.

But Montreal had beheld too many spectacles of a tragic sort, had grasped too much the gun and spade, to have any facility in mimic play.

Still the beaver fair was enlivened by music and tricksy gambols. Through all the ever opening and closing avenues a pageant went up and down, at which no colonist of New France could restrain his shouts of laughter,—a Dutchman with enormous stomach, long pipe, and short breeches, walking beside a lank and solemn Bostonnais. The two youths who had attired themselves for this masking were of Saint-Castin's train. That one who acted Puritan had drawn austere seams in his face with charcoal. His plain collar was severely turned down over a black doublet, which, with the sombre breeches and hose, had perhaps been stripped from some enemy that troubled Saint-Castin's border. The Bostonnais sung high shrill airs from a book he carried in one hand, only looking up to shake his head with cadaverous warning at his roaring spectators. One arm was linked in the Dutchman's, who took his pipe out of his mouth to say good-humoredly, "Ya-ya, ya-ya," to every sort of taunt. These types of rival colonies were such an exhilaration to the traders of New France that they pointed out the show to each other and pelted it with epithets all day.

La Salle came out of the palisade gate of the town, leading by the hand a frisking little girl. He restrained her from farther progress into the moving swarm, although she dragged his arm. "Thou canst here see all there is of it, Barbe. The nuns did well to oppose your looking on this roaring commerce. You should be housed within the Hôtel Dieu all this day, had I not spoken a careless word yesterday. You saw the governor's procession. To-morrow he will start on his return. And I with my men go to Fort Frontenac."

"**The beaver fair was enlivened by music and tricksy gambols.**"—
Page 59.

"And at day dawn naught of the Indians can be found," added Barbe, "except their ashes and litter and the broken flasks they leave. The trader's booths will also be empty and dirty."

"Come then, tiger-cat, return to thy cage."

"My uncle La Salle, let me look a moment longer. See that fat man and his lean brother the people are pointing at! Even the Indians jump and jeer. I would strike them for such insolence! There, my uncle La Salle, there is Monsieur Iron-hand talking to the ugly servant of Jeanne le Ber's father."

La Salle easily found Tonty. He was instructing and giving orders to several men collected for the explorer's service. Jolycœur,[6] his cap set on sidewise, was yet abashed in his impudence by the mastery of Tonty. He wore a new suit of buckskin, with the coureur de bois' red sash knotted around his waist.

"My uncle La Salle," inquired Barbe, turning over a disturbance in her mind, "must I live in the convent until I wed a man?"

"The convent is held a necessary discipline for young maids."

"I will then choose Monsieur Iron-hand directly. He would make a good husband."

"I think you are right," agreed La Salle.

"Because he would have but one hand to catch me with when I wished to run away," explained Barbe. "If he had also lost his feet it would be more convenient."

"The marriage between Monsieur de Tonty and Mademoiselle Barbe Cavelier may then be arranged?"

She looked at her uncle, answering his smile of amusement. But curving her neck from side to side, she still examined the Italian soldier.

"I can outrun most people," suggested Barbe; "but Monsieur de Tonty looks very tall and strong."

"Your intention is to take to the woods as soon as marriage sets you free?"

"My uncle La Salle, I do have such a desire to be free in the woods!"

"Have you, my child? If the wilderness thus draws you, you will sometime embrace it. Cavelier blood is wild juice."

"And could I take my fortune with me? If it cumbered I would leave it behind with Monsieur de Tonty or my brother."

"You will need all your fortune for ventures in the wilderness."

"And the fortunes of all your relatives and of as many as will give you credit besides," said a priest wearing the Sulpitian dress. He stopped before them and looked sternly at Barbe.

The Abbé Jean Cavelier had not such robust manhood as his brother. In him the Cavelier round lower lip and chin protruded, and the eyebrows hung forward.

La Salle had often felt that he stooped in conciliating Jean, when Jean held the family purse and doled out loans to an explorer always kept needy by great plans.

Jean had strongly the instinct of accumulation. He gauged the discovery and settlement of a continent by its promise of wealth to himself. His adherence to La Salle was therefore delicately adjusted by La Salle's varying fortunes; though at all times he gratified himself by handling with tyranny this younger and distinguished brother. Generous admiration of another's genius flowering from his stock with the perfect expression denied him, was scarcely possible in Jean Cavelier.

"The Sisters said I might come hither with my uncle La Salle," replied Barbe, to his unspoken rebuke.

"Into whose charge were your brother and yourself put when your parents died?"

"Into the charge of my uncle the Abbé Cavelier."

"Who brought your brother and you to this colony that he might watch over your nurture?"

"My uncle the Abbé Cavelier."

"It is therefore your uncle the Abbé Cavelier who will decide when to turn you out among Indians and traders."

"You carry too bitter a tongue, my brother Jean," observed La Salle. "The child has caught no harm. My own youth was cramped within religious walls."

"You carry too arrogant a mind now, my brother La Salle. I heard it noted of you to-day that you last night sat apart and deigned no word to them that have been of use to you in Montreal."

La Salle's face owned the sting. Shy natures have always been made to pay a tax on pride. But next to the slanderer we detest the bearer of his slander to our ears.

"It is too much for any man to expect in this world,—a brother who will defend him against his enemies."

As soon as this regret had burst from the explorer, he rested his look again on Tonty.

"I do defend you," asserted Abbé Cavelier; "and more than that I impoverish myself for you. But now that you come riding back from France on a high tide of the king's favor, I may not lay a correcting word on your haughty spirit. Neither yesterday nor to-day could I bring you to any reasonable state of humility. And all New France in full cry against you!"

Extreme impatience darkened La Salle's face; but without further reply he drew Barbe's hand and turned back with her toward the Hôtel Dieu. She had watched her uncle the Abbé wrathfully during his attack upon La Salle, but as he dropped his eyes no more to her level she was obliged to carry away her undischarged anger. This she did with a haughty bearing so like La Salle's that the Abbé grinned at it through his fretfulness.

He grew conscious of alien hair bristling against his neck as a voice mocked in undertone directly below his ear,—

"Yonder struts a great Bashaw that will sometime be laid low!"

The Abbé turned severely upon a person who presumed to tickle a priest's neck with his coarse mustache and astound a priest's ear with threats.

He recognized the man known as Jolycœur, who had been pushed against him in the throng. Jolycœur, by having his eyes fixed on the disappearing figure of La Salle, had missed the ear of the person he intended to reach. He recoiled from encountering the Abbé, whose wrath with sudden ebb ran back from a brother upon a brother's foes.

"You are the fellow I saw whining yesterday at Sieur de la Salle's heels. What hath the Sieur de la Salle done to any of you worthless woods-rangers, except give you labor and wages, when the bread you eat is a waste of his substance?"

Jolycœur, not daring to reply to a priest, slunk away in the crowd.

BOOK II.
FORT FRONTENAC.
1683 A. D.

I.
RIVAL MASTERS.

The gate of Fort Frontenac opened to admit several persons headed by a man who had a closely wrapped girl by his side. Before wooden palisades and walls of stone enclosed her, she turned her face to look across the mouth of Cataraqui River and at Lake Ontario rippling full of submerged moonlight. A magnified moon was rising. Farther than eye could reach it softened that northern landscape and provoked mystery in the shadows of the Thousand Islands.

South of the fort were some huts set along the margin of Ontario according to early French custom, which demanded a canoe highway in front of every man's door. West of these, half hid by forest, was an Indian village; and distinct between the two rose the huge white cross planted by Father Hennepin when he was first sent as missionary to Fort Frontenac.

An officer appeared beside the sentinel at the gate, and took off his hat before the muffled shape led first into his fortress. She bent her head for this civility and held her father's arm in silence. Canoemen and followers with full knowledge of the place moved on toward barracks or bakery. But the officer stopped their master, saying,—

"Monsieur le Ber, I have news for you."

"I have none for you," responded the merchant. "It is ever the same story,—men lost in the rapids and voyagers drenched to the skin. However, we had but one man drowned this time, and are only half dead of fatigue ourselves. Let us have some supper at once. What are your reports?"

"Monsieur, the Sieur de la Salle arrived here a few hours ago from the fort on the Illinois."

"The Sieur de la Salle?"

"Yes, monsieur."

"Why did you let him in?" demanded Le Ber, fiercely. "He hath no rights in this fortress now."

"His men were much exhausted, monsieur."

"He could have camped at the settlement."

"Monsieur, I wish to tell you at once that the last families have left the settlement."

"The Indians are yet there?"

"Yes, monsieur. But our settlers were afraid our Indians would join the other Iroquois."

"How many men had La Salle with him?"

"No more than half your party, monsieur. There was Jolycœur—"

"I tell you La Salle has no rights in this fort," interrupted Le Ber. "If he meddles with his merchandise stored here which the government has seized upon, I will arrest him."

"Yes, monsieur. The Father Louis Hennepin has also arrived from the wilderness after great peril and captivity."

"Tell me that La Salle's man Tonty is here! Tell me that there is a full muster of all the vagabonds from Michillimackinac! Tell me that Fort St. Louis of the Illinois hath moved on Fort Frontenac!"

The merchant's voice ascended a pyramid of vexation.

"No, monsieur. Monsieur de Tonty is not here. And the Father Louis Hennepin[7] only rests a few days before the fatigue of descending the rapids to Montreal. It was a grief to him to find his mission and the settlement so decayed after only five years' absence."

"Why do you fret me with the decay of the mission and breaking up of the settlement? If I were here as commandant of this fort I might then be blamed for its ruin. Perhaps my associates made a mistake in retaining an officer who had served under La Salle."

The commandant made no retort, but said,—

"Monsieur, I had almost forgotten to tell you we have another fair demoiselle within our walls to the honor of Fort Frontenac. The Abbé Cavelier with men from Lachine, arrived this morning, his young niece being with him. There are brave women in Montreal."

"That is right,—that is right!" exclaimed the irritable merchant. "Call all the Cavelier family hither and give up the fortress. I heard the Abbé had ventured ahead of me."

"Monsieur le Ber, what can they do against the king and the governor? Both king and governor have dispossessed La Salle. I admitted him as any wayfarer. The Abbé Cavelier came with a grievance against his brother. He hath lost money by him the same as others."

"Thou shalt not be kept longer in the night air," said Le Ber, with sudden tenderness to his daughter. "There is dampness within these walls to remind us of our drenchings in the rapids."

"We have fire in both upper and lower rooms of the officers' quarters," said the commandant.

They walked toward the long dwelling, their shadows stretching and blending over the ground.

"Where have you lodged these men?" inquired Le Ber.

The officer pointed to the barrack end of the structure made of hewed timbers. The wider portion intended for commandant's headquarters was built of stone, with Norman eaves and windows. Near the barracks stood a guardhouse. The bakery was at the opposite side of the gateway, and beyond it was the mill. La Salle had founded well this stronghold in the wilderness. Walls of hewed stone enclosed three sides, nine small cannon being mounted thereon.[8] Palisades were the defence on the water side. Fort Frontenac was built with four bastions. In two of these bastions were vaulted towers which served as magazines for ammunition.[9] A well was dug within the walls.

"Have you no empty rooms in the officers' quarters?"

The moon threw silhouette palisades on the ground, and made all these buildings cut blocks of shadow. There was a stir of evening wind in the forest all around.

"The men are in the barracks. But Sieur de la Salle is in the officers' house."

"May I ask you, Commandant," demanded Le Ber, "where you propose to lodge my daughter whom I have brought through the perils of the rapids, and cannot now return with?"

"Mademoiselle le Ber is most welcome to my own apartment, monsieur, and I will myself come downstairs."

"One near mine for yourself, monsieur. But with the Abbé and his niece and the boy and La Salle and Father Hennepin, to say no more, can we have many empty rooms? Father Hennepin is lodged downstairs, but La Salle hath his old room overlooking the river."

"How does he appear, Commandant?"

"Worn in his garb and very thin visaged, but unmoved by his misfortunes as a man of rock. Any one else would be prostrate and hopeless."

"A madman," pronounced Le Ber.

Careless laughter resounded from the barracks. Some water creature made so distinct a splash and struggle in Cataraqui River that imagination followed the widening circles spreading from its body until an island broke their huge circumference.

"See that something be sent us from the bakehouse," said Le Ber to the commandant, before leading his daughter into the quarters. "My men have brought provisions from Montreal."

"We can give you a good supper, monsieur. Two young deer were brought in to-day. As for Monsieur de la Salle," the commandant added, turning back from the door of the barracks, "you will perhaps not meet him at all in the officers' quarters. He ate and threw himself down at once to sleep, and he is in haste to set forward to Quebec."

The bakehouse was illuminated by its oven fire which shone with a dull crimson through the open door, but failed to find out dusky corners where bales, barrels, and cook's tools were stored. The oven was built in the wall, of stone and cement. The cook, a skipping little fellow smocked in white and wearing a cap, said to himself as he raked out coals and threw them in the fireplace,—

"What a waste of good material is this, when they glow and breathe with such ardor to roast some worthy martyr!"

"The beginning of a martyr is a saint," observed a soldier of the garrison, putting his fur-covered head between door and door-post in the little space he opened. "We have a saint just landed at Fort Frontenac."

He stepped in and shut the door, to lounge with the cook while the order he brought was obeyed.

"Some of the best you have, with a tender cut of venison, for Jacques le Ber and his daughter. And some salt meat for his men in the barracks."

The cook made light skips across the floor and returned with venison.

"Well-timed, my child; for the coals are ready, and so are my cakes for the oven. Le Ber is soon served. Get upon your knees by the hearth and watch this cut broil, while I slice the larding for the sore sides of these fellows that labored through the rapids."

When you are housed in a garrison the cook becomes a potentate; the soldier went willingly down as assistant.

"Are all the demoiselles of Montreal coming to Fort Frontenac?" inquired the cook, skipping around a great block on which lay a slab of cured meat, and nicely poising his knife-tip over it.

"That I cannot tell you," replied the soldier, beginning to perspire before the coals. "Le Ber's men have been talking in the barracks about this daughter of his. He brought her almost by force out of his house, where she has taken to shutting herself in her own room."

"I have heard of this demoiselle," said the cook. "May the saints incline more women to shut themselves up at home!"

"She is his favorite child. He brought her on this dangerous voyage to wean her from too much praying."

"Too much praying!" exclaimed the cook.

"He desires to have her look more on the world, lest she should die of holiness," explained the soldier.

"Turn that venison," shouted the cook. "Was there ever a saint who liked burnt meat? I could lift this Jacques le Ber on a hot fork for dragging out a woman who inclined to stay praying in the house. Some men are stone blind to the blessings of Heaven!"

II.
A TRAVELLED FRIAR.

The lower room of the officers' lodging was filled with the light of a fire. To the hearth was drawn a half-circle of men, their central figure being a Récollet friar, so ragged and weather-stained that he seemed some ecclesiastical scarecrow placed there to excite laughter and tears in his beholders.

This group arose as Jacques le Ber entered with his daughter, and were eager to be of service to her.

"There is a fire lighted in the hall upstairs by which mademoiselle can sit," said the sergeant of the fort.

Le Ber conducted her to the top of a staircase which ascended the side of the room before he formally greeted any one present. He returned, unwinding his saturated wool wrappings and pulling off his cap of beaver skin. He was a swarthy man with anxious and calculating wrinkles between his eyebrows.

"Do I see Father Hennepin?" exclaimed Le Ber, squaring his mouth, "or is this a false image of him set before me?"

"You see Father Hennepin," the friar responded with dignity,—"explorer, missionary among the Sioux, and sufferer in the cause of religion."

"How about that hunger for adventure,—hast thou appeased it?" inquired Le Ber with freedom of manner he never assumed toward any other priest.

The merchant stood upon the hearth steaming in front of the tattered Récollet, who from his seat regarded his half-enemy with a rebuking eye impressive to the other men.

"Jacques le Ber, my son, while your greedy hands have been gathering money, the poor Franciscan has baptized heathen, discovered and explored rivers; he has lived the famished life of a captive, and come nigh death in many ways. I have seen a great waterfall five hundred feet high, whereunder four carriages might pass abreast without being wet. I have depended for food on what Heaven sent. Vast fish are to be found in the waters of that western land, and there also you may see beasts having manes and hoofs and horns, to frighten a Christian."

"And what profit doth La Salle get out of all this?" inquired Le Ber, spreading his legs before the fire as he looked down at Father Hennepin.

"What I have accomplished has been done for the spread of the faith, and not for the glory of Monsieur de la Salle, who has treated me badly."

"Does he ever treat any one well?" exclaimed Le Ber. "Does not every man in his service want to shoot him?"

"He has an over-haughty spirit, which breaks out into envy of men like me," admitted the good Fleming, whose weather-seamed face and plump lips glowed with conscious greatness before the fire. "I have decided to avoid further encounter with Monsieur de la Salle while we both remain at Fort Frontenac, for my mind is set on peace, and it is true where Monsieur de la Salle appears there can be no peace."

Jacques le Ber turned himself to face the chimney.

"Thou hast no doubt accomplished a great work, Father Hennepin," he said, with the immediate benevolence a man feels toward one who has reached his point of view. "When I have had supper with my daughter I will sit down here and beg you to tell me all that befell your wanderings, and what savages they were who received the faith at your hands, and how the Sieur de la Salle hath turned even a Récollet Father against himself."

"Perhaps Father Hennepin will tell about his buffalo hunt," suggested the sergeant of the fortress, "and how he headed a wounded buffalo from flight and drove it back to be shot."[10]

Father Hennepin looked down at patches of buffalo hide which covered holes in his habit. He remembered the trampling of a furious beast's hoofs and the twitch of its short sharp horn in his folds of flesh as it lifted him. He remembered his wounds and the soreness of his bones which lasted for months, yet his lips parted over happy teeth and he roared with laughter.

III.
HEAVEN AND EARTH.

Jeanne le Ber sat down upon a high-backed bench before the fire in the upper room. This apartment was furnished and decorated only by abundant firelight, which danced on stone walls and hard dark rafters, on rough floor and high enclosure, of the stairway. At opposite sides of the room were doors which Jeanne did not know opened into chambers scarcely larger than the sleepers who might lodge therein.

She sat in strained thought, without unwrapping herself, though shudders were sent through her by damp raiment. When her father came up with the sergeant who carried their supper, he took off her cloak, smoothed her hair, and tenderly reproved her. He set the dishes on the bench between them, and persuaded Jeanne to eat what he carved for her,—a swarthy nurse whose solicitude astounded the soldier.

Another man came up and opened the door nearest the chimney, on that side which overlooked the fortress enclosure. He paused in descending, loaded with the commandant's possessions, to say that this bedroom was designed for mademoiselle, and was now ready.

"And thou must get to it as soon as the river's chill is warmed out of thy bones," said Le Ber. "I will sit and hear the worthy friar downstairs tell his strange adventures. The sound of your voice can reach me with no effort whatever. My bedroom will be next yours, or near by, and no harm can befall you in Fort Frontenac."

Jeanne kissed his cheek before he returned to the lower room, and when the supper was removed she sat drying herself by the fire.

The eager piety of her early girlhood, which was almost fantastic in its expression, had yet worked out a nobly spiritual face. She was a beautiful saint.

For several years Jeanne le Ber had refused the ordinary clothing of women. Her visible garment was made of a soft fine blanket of white wool, with long sleeves falling nearly to her feet. It was girded to her waist by a cord from which hung her rosary. Her neck stood slim and white above the top of this robe, without ornament except the peaked monk's hood which hung behind it.

This creature like a flame of living white fire stood up and turned her back to the ruddier logs, and clasped her hands across the top of her head. Her eyes wasted scintillations on rafters while she waited for heavenly peace to calm the strong excitement driving her.

The door of Jeanne's chamber stood open as the soldier had left it. At the opposite side of the room a similar door opened, and La Salle came out. He moved a step, toward the hearth, but stopped, and the pallor of a swoon filled his face.

"Sieur de la Salle," said Jeanne in a whisper. She let her arms slip down by her sides. The eccentric robe with its background of firelight cast her up tall and white before his eyes.

In the explorer's most successful moments he had never appeared so majestic. Though his dress was tarnished by the wilderness, he had it carefully arranged; for he liked to feel it fitting him with an exactness which would not annoy his thoughts.

No formal greeting preluded the crash of this encounter between La Salle and Jeanne le Ber. What had lain repressed by prayer and penance, or had been trodden down league by league in the wilds, leaped out with strength made mighty by such repression.

Voices in loud and merry conversation below and occasional laughter came up the open stairway and made accompaniment to this half-hushed duet.

"Jeanne," stammered La Salle.

"Sieur de la Salle, I was just going to my room."

She moved away from him to the side of the hearth, as he advanced and sat down upon the bench. Unconscious that she stood while he was sitting, as if overcome by sudden blindness he reached toward her with a groping gesture.

"Take hold of my hand, Sainte Jeanne."

"And if I take hold of your hand, Sieur de la Salle," murmured the girl, bending toward him though she held her arms at her sides, "what profit will it be to either of us?"

"I beg that you will take hold of my hand."

Her hand, quivering to each finger tip, moved out and met and was clasped in his. La Salle's head dropped on his breast.

Jeanne turned away her face. Voices and laughter jangled in the room below. In this silent room pulse answered pulse, and with slow encounter eyes answered the adoration of eyes. In terror of herself Jeanne uttered the whispered cry,—

"I am afraid!"

She veiled herself with the long sleeve of her robe.

"And of what should you be afraid when we are thus near together?" said La Salle. "The thing to be afraid of is losing this. Such gladness has been long coming; for I was a man when you were born, Sainte Jeanne."

"Let go my hand, Sieur de la Salle."

"Do you want me to let it go, Sainte Jeanne?"

"No, Sieur de la Salle."

Dropping her sleeve Jeanne faced heaven through the rafters. Tears stormed down her face, and her white throat swelled with strong repressed sobs. Like some angel caught in a snare, she whispered her up-directed wail,—

"All my enormity must now be confessed! Whenever Sieur de la Salle has been assailed my soul rose up in arms for him. Oh, my poor father! So dear has Sieur de la Salle been to me that I hated the hatred of my father. What shall I do to tear out this awful love? I have fought it through midnights and solitary days of ceaseless prayer. Oh, Sieur de la Salle, why art thou such a man? Pray to God and invoke the saints for me, and help me to go free from this love!"

"Jeanne," said La Salle, "you are so holy I dare touch no more than this sweet hand. It fills me with life. Ask me not to pray to God that he will take the life from me. Oh, Jeanne, if you could reach out of your eternity of devotion and hold me always by the hand, what a man I might be!"

She dropped her eyes to his face, saying like a soothing mother,—

"Thou greatest and dearest, there is a gulf between us which we cannot pass. I am vowed to Heaven. Thou art vowed to great enterprises. The life of the family is not for us. If God showed me my way by thy side I would go through any wilderness. But Jeanne was made to listen in prayer and silence and secrecy and anguish for the word of Heaven. The worst is,"—her stormy sob again shook her from head to foot,—"you will be at court, and beautiful women will love the great explorer. And one will shine; she will be set like a star as high as the height of being your wife. And Jeanne,—oh, Jeanne! here in this rough, new world,—she must eternally learn to be nothing!"

"My wife!" said La Salle, turning her hand in his clasp, and laying his cheek in her palm. "You are my wife. There is no court. There is no world to discover. There is only the sweet, the rose-tender palm of my wife where I can lay my tired cheek and rest."

Jeanne's fingers moved with involuntary caressing along the lowest curve of his face.

An ember fell on the hearth beside them, and Father Hennepin emphasized some point in his relation with a stamp of his foot.

"You left a glove at my father's house, Sieur de la Salle, and I hid it; I put my face to it. And when I burned it, my own blood seemed to ooze out of that crisping glove."

La Salle trembled. The dumb and solitary man was dumb and solitary in his love.

"Now we must part," breathed Jeanne. "Heaven is strangely merciful to sinners. I never could name you to my confessor or show him this formless anguish; but now that it has been owned and cast out, my heart is glad."

La Salle rose up and stood by the hearth. As she drew her hand from his continued hold he opened his arms. Jeanne stepped backward, her eyes swarming with motes of light. She turned and reached her chamber door; but as the saint receded from temptation the woman rose in strength. She ran to La Salle, and with a tremor and a sob in his arms, met his mouth with the one kiss of her life. As suddenly she ran from him and left him.

La Salle had had his sublime moment of standing at the centre of the universe and seeing all things swing around him, which comes to every one successful in embodying a vast idea. But from this height he looked down at that experience.

He stood still after Jeanne's door closed until he felt his own intrusion. This drove him downstairs and out of the house, regardless of Jacques le Ber, Father Hennepin, and the officers of the fortress, who turned to gaze at his transit.

Proud satisfaction, strange in a ruined man, appeared on the explorer's face. He felt his reverses as cobwebs to be brushed away. He was loved. The king had been turned against him. His enemies had procured Count Frontenac's removal, and La Barre the new governor, conspiring to seize his estate, had ruined his credit. But he was loved. Even on this homeward journey an officer had passed him with authority to take possession of his new post on the Illinois River. His discoveries were doubted and sneered at, as well as half claimed by boasting subordinates, who knew nothing about his greater views. Yet the only softener of this man of noble granite was a spirit-like girl, who regarded the love of her womanhood as sin.

La Salle stood in the midst of enemies. He stood considering merely how his will should break down the religious walls Jeanne built around herself, and how Jacques le Ber might be conciliated by shares in the profits of the

West. Behind stretched his shadowed life, full of misfortune; good was held out to him to be withdrawn at the touch of his fingers. But this good he determined to have; and thinking of her, La Salle walked the stiffened frost-crisp ground of the fortress half the night.

IV.
A CANOE FROM THE ILLINOIS.

When Barbe Cavelier awoke next morning and saw around her the stone walls of Fort Frontenac instead of a familiar convent enclosure, she sat up in her bed and laughed aloud. The tiny cell echoed. Never before had laughter of young girl been heard there. And when she placed her feet upon the floor perhaps their neat and exact pressure was a surprise to battered planks used to the smiting tread of men.

Barbe proceeded to dress herself, with those many curvings of neck and figure, which, in any age, seem necessary to the fit sitting of a young maid in her garments. Her aquiline face glowed, full of ardent life.

Some raindrops struck the roof-window and ran down its panes like tears. When Barbe had considered her astounding position as the only woman in Fort Frontenac, and felt well compacted for farther adventures, she sprung upon the bunk, and stood with her head near the roof, looking out into the fortress and its adjacent world. Among moving figures she could not discern her uncle La Salle, or her uncle the Abbé, or even her brother. These three must be yet in the officers' house. Dull clouds were scudding. As Barbe opened the sash and put her head out the morning air met her with a chill. Fort Frontenac's great walls half hid an autumn forest, crowding the lake's distant border in measureless expanse of sad foliage. Eastward, she caught ghostly hints of islands on misty water. The day was full of depression. Ontario stood up against the sky, a pale greenish fleece, raked at intervals by long wires of rain.

But such influences had no effect on a healthy warm young creature, freed unaccountably from her convent, and brought on a perilous, delightful journey to so strange a part of her world.

She noticed a parley going forward at the gate. Some outsider demanded entrance, for the sentry disappeared between the towers and returned for orders. He approached the commandant who stood talking with Jacques le Ber, the merchant of Montreal. Barbe could see Le Ber's face darken. With shrugs and negative gestures he decided against the newcomer, and the sentinel again disappeared to refuse admission. She wondered if a band of Iroquois waited outside. Among Abbé Cavelier's complaints of La Salle was Governor la Barre's accusation that La Salle stirred enmity in the Iroquois by protecting the Illinois tribe they wished to exterminate.

"Even these Indians on the lake shore," meditated Barbe, "who settled there out of friendship to my uncle La Salle, may turn against him and try to harm him as every one does now that his fortunes are low. I would be a man faithful to my friend, if I were a man at all."

She watched for a sight of the withdrawing party on the lake, and presently a large canoe holding three men shot out beyond the walls. One stood erect, gazing back at the fort with evident anxiety. Neither the smearing medium of damp weather nor increasing distance could rob Barbe of that man's identity. His large presence, his singular carriage of the right arm, even his features sinking back to space, stamped him Henri de Tonty.

"He has come here to see my uncle La Salle, and they have refused to let him enter," she exclaimed aloud.

Stripping a coverlet from her berth she whipped the outside air with it until the crackle brought up a challenge from below.

Fort Frontenac was a seignorial rather than a military post, and its discipline had been lax since the governor's Associates seized it, yet a sentinel paced this morning before the officers' quarters. When he saw the signal withdrawn and a lovely face with dark eyelashes and a topknot of curls looking down at him, he could do nothing but salute it, and Barbe shut her window.

Dropping in excitement from the bunk, she ran across the upper room to knock at La Salle's door.

A boy stood basking in solitude by the chimney.

Her uncle La Salle's apartment seemed filled with one strong indignant voice, leaking through crevices and betraying its matter to the common hall.

"You may knock there until you faint of hunger," remarked the lad at the hearth. "I also want my breakfast, but these precious Associates will let us starve in the fort they have stolen before they dole us out any food. I would not mind going into the barracks and messing, but I have you also to consider."

"It is not anything to eat, Colin—it is pressing need of my uncle La Salle!"

"The Abbé has pressing need of our uncle La Salle. It was great relief to catch him here at Frontenac. I have heard every bit of the lecture: what amounts our uncle the Abbé has ventured in western explorations; and what a fruitless journey he has made here to rescue for himself some of the stores of this fortress; and what danger all we Caveliers stand in of being poisoned on account of my uncle La Salle, so that the Abbé can scarce trust us out of his sight, even with nuns guarding you."

To Barbe's continued knocking her guardian made the curtest reply. He opened the door, looked at her sternly, saying, "Go away, mademoiselle," and shut it tightly again.

She ran back to her lookout and was able to discern the same canoe moving off on the lake.

"Colin," demanded Barbe, wrapping herself, "You must run with me."

"Certainly, mademoiselle, and I trust you are making haste toward a table."

"We must run outside the fortress."

Though the boy felt it a grievance that he should follow instead of lead to any adventure, he dashed heartily out with her, intending to take his place when he understood the action. Rain charged full in their faces. The sentry was inclined to hold them at the fortress gate until he had orders, and Barbe's impatience darted from her eyes.

"You will get me into trouble," he said. "This gate has been swinging overmuch lately."

"Let us out," persuaded Colin. "The Associates will not care what becomes of a couple of Caveliers."

"Where are you going?"

"My sister wishes to run to the Iroquois village," responded Colin, "and beg there for a little sagamite. We get nothing to eat in Fort Frontenac."

The soldier laughed.

"If you are going to the Iroquois village why don't you say your errand is to Catharine Tegahkouita? It is no sin to ask an Indian saint's prayers."

Barbe formed her lips to inquire, "Has Tegahkouita come to Fort Frontenac?" But this impulse passed into discreet silence, and the man let them out.

They ran along the palisades southward, Barbe keeping abreast of Colin though she made skimming dips as the swallow flies, and with a détour quite to the lake's verge, avoided the foundation of an outwork.

Father Hennepin's cross stood up, a huge white landmark between habitant settlement on the lake, and Indian village farther west but visible through the clearing. Ontario seemed to rise higher and top the world, its green curves breaking at their extremities into white spatter, the one boat in sight making deep obeisance to heaving water.

"Do you see a canoe riding yonder?" exclaimed Barbe to Colin, as they ran along wet sand.

"Any one may see a canoe riding yonder. Was it to race with that canoe we came out, mademoiselle?"

"Wave your arms and make signals to the men in it, Colin. They must be stopped. I am sure that one is Monsieur de Tonty, and they were turned away from the fortress gate. They have business with our uncle La Salle, and see how far they have gone before we could get out ourselves!"

"Why, then, did you follow?" demanded her brother, waving his arms and flinging his cap in the rain. "They may have business with our uncle La Salle, but they have no business with a girl. This was quite my affair, Mademoiselle Cavelier."

A maid whose feet were heavy with the mud of a once ploughed clearing could say little in praise of such floundering. She paid no attention to Colin's rebuke, but watched for the canoe to turn landward. Satisfied that it was heading toward them, Barbe withdrew from the border of the lake. She would not shelter herself in any deserted hut of the habitant village. Colin followed her in vexation to Father Hennepin's mission house, remonstrating as he skipped, and turning to watch the canoe with rain beating his face.

They found the door open. The floor was covered with sand blown there, and small stones cast by the hands of irreverent passing Indian boys. The chapel stood a few yards away, but this whole small settlement was dominated by its cross.[11]

Barbe and Colin were scarcely under this roof shelter before Tonty strode up to the door. He took off his hat with the left hand, his dark face bearing the rain like a hardy flower. Dangers, perpetual immersion in Nature, and the stimulus of vast undertakings had so matured Tonty that Barbe felt more awe of his buckskin presence than her memory of the fine young soldier in Montreal could warrant. She wanted to look at him and say nothing. Colin, who knew this soldier only by reputation, was eager to meet and urge him into Father Hennepin's house.

Tonty's reluctant step crunched sand on the boards. He kept his gaze upon Barbe and inquired,—

"Have I the honor, mademoiselle, to address the niece of Monsieur de la Salle?"

"The niece and nephew of Monsieur de la Salle," put forth Colin.

"Yes, monsieur. You may remember me as the young tiger-cat who sprung upon my uncle La Salle when you arrived with him from France."

"I never forgot you, mademoiselle. You so much resemble Monsieur de la Salle."

"It is on his account we have run out of the fort to stop you. He does not know you are here. I saw the sentinel close the gate against some one, and afterward your boat pushed out."

"And did you shake a signal from an upper window in the fort?"

"Monsieur, I could not be sure that you saw it, though I could see your boat."

"She made it very much her affair," observed Colin, with the merciless disapproval of a lad. "Monsieur de Tonty, there was no use in her trampling through sand and rain like a Huron witch going to some herb gathering. It was my business to do the errand of my uncle La Salle. When she goes back she will get a lecture and a penance, for all her sixteen years."

"Mademoiselle," said Tonty, "I am distressed if my withdrawal from Fort Frontenac causes you trouble. I meant to camp here. I was determined to see Monsieur de la Salle."

"Monsieur," courageously replied Barbe, "you cause me no trouble at all. I thought you were returning to your fort on the Illinois. I did not stop to tell my brother, but made him run with me. It is a shame that the enemies of my uncle La Salle hold you out of Fort Frontenac."

"But very little would you get to eat there," consoled young Cavelier. "We have had nothing to break our fast on this morning."

"Then let us get ready some breakfast for you," proposed Tonty, as his men entered with the lading of the canoe. They had stopped at the doorstep, but Father Hennepin's hewed log house contained two rooms, and he pointed them to the inner one. There they let down their loads, one man, a surgeon, remaining, and the other, a canoeman, going out again in search of fuel.

"Monsieur, it would be better for us to hurry back to the fortress and call my uncle La Salle."

"Nothing will satisfy you, mademoiselle," denounced Colin. "Out you must come to stop Monsieur de Tonty. Now back you must go through weather which is not fitting for any demoiselle to face."

"Mademoiselle," said Tonty, "if you return now it will be my duty to escort you as far as the fortress gate."

Barbe drew her wrappings over her face, as he had seen a wild sensitive plant fold its leaves and close its cups.

"I will retire to the chapel and wait there until my uncle La Salle comes," she decided, "and my brother must run to call him."

"You may take to sanctuary as soon as you please," responded Colin, "and I will attend to my uncle La Salle's business. But the first call I make shall be upon the cook in this camp."

V.
FATHER HENNEPIN'S CHAPEL.

Tonty held a buffalo robe over Barbe during her quick transit from cabin to church. Its tanned side was toward the weather, and its woolly side continued to comfort her after she was under shelter. Tonty bestowed it around her and closed the door again, leaving her in the dim place.

Father Hennepin's deserted chapel was of hewed logs like his dwelling. A rude altar remained, but without any ornaments, for the Récollet had carried these away to his western mission. Some unpainted benches stood in a row. The roof could be seen through rafters, and drops of rain with reiterating taps fell along the centre of the floor. A chimney of stones and cement was built outside the chapel, of such a size that its top yawned like an open cell for rain, snow, or summer sunshine. Within, it spread a generous hearth and an expanse of grayish fire-wall little marked by the blue incense which rises from burning wood.

Barbe looked briefly around the chapel. She laid the buffalo hide before the altar and knelt upon it.

Tonty returned with a load of fuel and busied himself at the fireplace. The boom of the lake, and his careful stirring and adjusting in ancient ashes, made a background to her silence. Yet she heard through her devotions every movement he made, and the low whoop peculiar to flame when it leaps to existence and seizes its prey.

A torrent of fire soon poured up the flue. Tonty grasped a brush made of wood shavings, remnant of Father Hennepin's housekeeping, and whirled dust and litter in the masculine fashion. When he left the chapel it glowed with the resurrected welcome it had given many a primitive congregation of Indians and French settlers, when the lake beat up icy winter foam.

Beside the fireplace was a window so high that its log sill met Barbe's chin as she looked out. Jutting roof and outer chimney wall made a snug spot like a sentry-box without. She dried her feet, holding them one at a time to the red hot glow, and glanced through this window at the mission house's sodden logs and crumbled chinking. The excitement of her sally out of Fort Frontenac died away. She felt distressed because she had come, and faint for her early convent breakfast.

She saw Tonty through the window carrying a dish carefully covered. He approached the broken pane, and Barbe eagerly helped him to unfasten the sash and swing it out. In doing this, Tonty held her platter braced by his iron-handed arm.

The fare was passed in to her without apology, and she received it with sincere gratitude, afterward drawing a bench near the fire and sitting down in great privacy and comfort.

The moccasins of a frontiersman could make no sound above flap of wind and pat of water. Tonty paced from window to chapel front, believing that he kept out of Barbe's sight. But after an interval he was amused to see, rising over the sill within, a topknot of curls, and eyes filled with the alert, shy spirit of the deer whose flesh she had just eaten.

For some reason this scrutiny of Barbe's made him regret that he had lain aside the gold and white uniform of France, and the extreme uses to which his gauntlets had been put. Entrenched behind logs she unconsciously poured the fires of her youth upon Tonty.

Not only was one pane in the sash gone, but all were shattered, giving easy access to his voice as he stood still and explained.

"Frontenac is a lonely post, mademoiselle. It is necessary for you to have a sentinel."

"Yes, monsieur; you are very good." Barbe accepted the fact with lowered eyelids. "Has my brother yet gone to call my uncle La Salle?"

"Yes, mademoiselle. As soon as we could give him some breakfast he set out."

"Colin is a gourmand. All very young people gormandize more or less," remarked Barbe, with a sense of emancipation from the class she condemned.

"I hope you could eat what I brought you?"

"It was quite delicious, monsieur. I ate every bit of it."

The boom of the lake intruded between their voices. Barbe's black eyelashes flickered sensitively upon her cheeks, and Tonty, feeling that he looked too steadily at her, dropped his eyes to his folded arms.

"Monsieur de Tonty," inquired Barbe, appealing to experience, "do you think sixteen years very young?"

"It is the most charming age in the world, mademoiselle."

"Monsieur, I mean young for maturing one's plan of life."

"That depends upon the person," replied Tonty. "At sixteen I was revolting against the tyranny which choked Italy. And I was an exile from my country before the age of twenty, mademoiselle."

Barbe gazed straight at Tonty, her gray eyes firing like opals with enthusiasm.

"And my uncle La Salle at sixteen was already planning his discoveries. Monsieur, I also have my plans. Many missionaries must be needed among the Indians."

"You do not propose going as a missionary among the Indians, mademoiselle?"

Barbe critically examined his smile. She evaded his query.

"Are the Indian women beautiful, Monsieur de Tonty?"

"They do not appear so to me, mademoiselle, though the Illinois are a straight and well-made race."

"You must find it a grand thing to range that western country."

"But in the midst of our grandeur the Iroquois threaten us even there. How would mademoiselle like to mediate between these invaders and the timid Illinois, suspected by one tribe and threatened by the other; to carry the wampum belt of peace on the open field between two armies, and for your pains get your scalp-lock around the fingers of a Seneca chief and his dagger into your side?"

"Oh, monsieur!" whispered Barbe, flushing with the wild pinkness of roses on the plains, "what amusements you do have in the great west! And is it a castle on a mountain, that Fort St. Louis of the Illinois?"

"A stockade on a cliff, mademoiselle."

Tonty felt impelled to put himself nearer this delicate head set with fine small ears and quartered by the angles of the window-frame. When she meditated, her lashes and brows and aquiline curves and gray tones flushing to rose were delightful to a wilderness-saturated man. But he held to his strict position as sentinel.

"Monsieur," said Barbe, "there is something on my mind which I will tell you. I was thinking of the new world my uncle La Salle discovered, even before you came to Montreal. Now I think constantly of Fort St. Louis of the Illinois. Monsieur, I dream of it,—I go in long journeys and never arrive; I see it through clouds, and wide rivers flow between it and me; and I am homesick. Yes, monsieur, that is the strangest thing,—I have cried of homesickness for Fort St. Louis of the Illinois!"

"Mademoiselle," said Tonty, his voice vibrating, "there is a stranger thing. It is this,—that a man with a wretched hand of iron should suddenly find within himself a heart of fire!"

When this confession had burst from him he turned his back without apology, and Barbe's forehead sunk upon the window-sill.

Within the chapel, drops from the cracked roof still fell in succession, like invisible fingers playing scales along the boards. Outside was the roar of the landlocked sea, and the higher music of falling rain. Barbe let her furtive eyes creep up the sill and find Tonty's large back on which she looked with abashed but gratified smiles.

"Mademoiselle," he begged without turning, "forgive what I have said."

"Certainly, monsieur," she responded. "What was it that you said?"

"Nothing, mademoiselle, nothing."

"Then, monsieur, I forgive you for saying nothing."

Tonty, in his larger perplexity at having made such a confession without La Salle's leave, missed her sting.

Nothing more was said through the window. Barbe moved back, and the stalwart soldier kept his stern posture; until La Salle, whose approach had been hidden by chimney and mission house, burst abruptly into view. As he came up, both he and Tonty opened their arms. Strong breast to strong breast, cheek touching cheek, spare olive-hued man and dark rich-blooded man hugged each other.

Barbe's convent lessons of embroidery and pious lore had included no heathen tales of gods or heroes. Yet to her this sight was like a vision of two great cloudy figures stalking across the world and meeting with an embrace.

VI.
LA SALLE AND TONTY.

When one of the men had been called from the mission house to stand guard, they came directly into the chapel, preferring to talk there in the presence of Barbe.

La Salle kissed her hand and her cheek, and she sat down before the fire, spreading the buffalo skin under her feet.

As embers sunk and the talk of the two men went on, she crept as low as this shaggy carpet, resting arms and head upon the bench. The dying fire made exquisite color in this dismal chapel.

"The governor's man, when he arrived to seize Fort St. Louis, gave you my letter of instructions, Tonty?"

"Yes, Monsieur de la Salle."

"Then, my lad, why have you abandoned the post and followed me? You should have stayed to be my representative. They have Frontenac. Crévecœur was ruined for us. If they get St. Louis of the Illinois entirely into their hands they will claim the whole of Louisiana, these precious Associates."

Tonty, laying his sound arm across his commandant's shoulder, exclaimed, "Monsieur, I have followed you five hundred leagues to drag that rascal Jolycœur back with me. He told at Fort St. Louis that this should be your last journey."

La Salle laughed.

"Let me tie Jolycœur and fling him into my canoe, and I turn back at once. I can hold your claims on the Illinois against any number of governor's agents. Take the surgeon Liotot in Jolycœur's place. Liotot came with me, anxious to return to France."

"Jolycœur is no worse than the others, my Tonty, and he has had many opportunities. How often has my life been threatened!"

"He intends mischief, monsieur. If I had heard it before you set out, this journey need not have been made."

"Tonty," declared the explorer, "I think sometimes I carry my own destruction within myself. I will not chop nice phrases for these hounds who continually ruin my undertakings by their faithlessness. If a man must keep patting the populace, he can do little else. But I am glad you overtook me here. My Tonty, if I had a hundred men like you I could spread out the unknown wilderness and possess it as that child possesses that hide of buffalo."

Though their undertakings were united, and the Italian had staked his fortune in the Norman's ventures, La Salle always assumed, and Tonty from the first granted him, entire mastery of the West. Both looked with occupied eyes at Barbe, who felt her life enlarged by witnessing this conference.

"Monsieur, what aspect have affairs taken since you reached Fort Frontenac?"

"Worse, Tonty, than I dreaded when I left the Illinois. You know how this new governor stripped Fort Frontenac of men and made its unprotected state an excuse for seizing it, saying I had not obeyed the king's order to maintain a garrison. And you know how he and the merchants of Montreal have possessed themselves of my seigniory here. They have sold and are still busy selling my goods from this post, putting the money into their pockets. I spent nearly thirty-five thousand francs improving this grant of Frontenac. But worse than that, Tonty, they have ruined my credit both here and in France. Even my brother will no more lift a finger for me. The king is turned against me. The fortunes of my family—even the fortune of that child—are sucked down in my ruin."

Barbe noted her own bankruptcy with the unconcern of youth. Monsieur de Tonty's face, when you looked up at it from a rug beside the hearth, showed well its full rounded chin, square jaws, and high temples, the richness of its Italian coloring against the blackness of its Italian hair.

"They call me a dreamer and a madman, these fellows now in power, and have persuaded the king that my discoveries are of no account."

"Monsieur," exclaimed Tonty, "do you remember the mouth of the great river?"[12]

Face glowed opposite face as they felt the log walls roll away from environing their vision. It was no longer the wash of the Ontario they heard, but the voice of the Mexican gulf. The yellow flood of Mississippi poured out between marsh borders. Again discharges of musketry seemed to shake the morasses beside a naked water world, the Te Deum to arise, and the explorer to be heard proclaiming,—

"In the name of the most high, mighty, invincible, and victorious Prince, Louis the Great, by the grace of God king of France and of Navarre, Fourteenth of that name, I, this ninth day of April, one thousand and six hundred and eighty-two, in virtue of the commission of his Majesty, which

I hold in my hand and which may be seen by all whom it may concern, have taken and do now take, in the name of his Majesty and of his successors to the crown, possession of this country of Louisiana, the seas, harbors, ports, bays, adjacent straits, and all the nations, people, provinces, cities, towns, villages, mines, minerals, fisheries, streams, and rivers within the extent of the said Louisiana, from the mouth of the great river St. Louis, otherwise called the Ohio, as also along the river Colbert or Mississippi, and the rivers which discharge themselves thereinto, from its source beyond the country of the Nadouessioux, as far as its mouth at the sea, or Gulf of Mexico."[13]

"Monsieur," exclaimed Tonty, "the plunderers of your fortune cannot take away that discovery or blot out the world you then opened. And what is Europe compared to this vast country? At the height of his magnificence Louis cannot picture to himself the grandeur of this western empire. France is but the palm of his hand beside it. It stretches from endless snow to endless heat; its breadth no man may guess. Nearly all the native tribes affiliate readily with the French. We have to dispute us only the English who hold a little strip by the ocean, the Dutch with smaller holding inland, and a few Spaniards along the Gulf."

"And all may be driven out before the arms of France," exclaimed La Salle. "These crawling merchants and La Barre,—soldier, he calls himself!—see nothing of this. Every man for his own purse among them. But thou seest it, Tonty. I see it. And we are no knights on a crusade. Nor are we unpractised courtiers shredding our finery away on the briers of the wilderness. This western enterprise is based on geographical facts. No mind can follow all the development of that rich land. It is an empire," declared La Salle, striding between hearth and chancel-rail, unconscious that he lifted his voice to the rafters of a sanctuary, "which Louis might drop France itself to grasp!"

"The king will be convinced of this, Monsieur de la Salle, when you again have his ear. When you have showed him what streams of commerce must flow out through a post stationed at the mouth of the Mississippi. France will then have a cord drawn half around this country."

"Tonty, if you could be commandant of every fort I build, navigator of every ship I set afloat, if you could live in every man who labors for me, if you could stand forever between those Iroquois wolves and the tribes we try to band for mutual protection, and at the same time, if you could always be at my side to ward off gun, knife, and poison,—you would make me the most successful man on earth."

"I have travelled five hundred leagues to ward poison away from you, monsieur. And you laugh at me."

**"Tonty, if you could be commandant of every fort I build," etc.—
Page 124.**

"For your pains, I will dismiss Jolycœur to-day, and take Liotot with me."

"And will you come here as soon as you dismiss him and let my men prepare your food?"

"Willingly. Fort Frontenac, with my rights in it denied, is no halting place for me. To-morrow I set out again to France, and you to the fort on the Illinois. But, Tonty—"

La Salle's face relaxed into tenderness as he laid his hands upon his friend's shoulders. The Italian's ardent temperament was the only agent which ever fused and made facile of tongue and easy of confidence that man of cold reserve known as La Salle. The Italian guessed what he had to say. They both glanced at Barbe and flushed. But the nebulous thought surrounding the name of Jeanne le Ber was never condensed to spoken word.

Tonty's sentinel opened the chapel door and broke up this council. He said an Indian stood there with him demanding to be admitted.

VII.
AN ADOPTION.

"What does he want?" inquired Tonty.

"He is determined to speak with you, Monsieur de Tonty, from what I can gather out of his words."

"Let him wait in the mission house, then," said Tonty, "until Monsieur de la Salle has ended his business."

"I have ended," said La Salle. "It is time I ordered my men and baggage and canoes out of Fort Frontenac."

"Monsieur, remain, and let an order from you be taken to the gate."

"Some of those sulky fellows need my hand over them, Tonty. Besides, there are matters which must be definitely settled before I leave the fort. I have need to go myself, besides the obligation to deliver this runaway girl, on whom her uncle La Salle is always bringing penances."

Barbe sprung up and put herself in the attitude of accompanying him.

"Mademoiselle," said Tonty, "the rain is still falling. If Monsieur de la Salle can carry this hide over you, it will be some protection."

He took up the buffalo skin, and shook it to loosen any dust which might be clinging to the shag.

"Monsieur, you are very good," she answered. "But it is not necessary for me."

"Mademoiselle cares very little about a wetting," said La Salle. "She was born to be a princess of the backwoods. Call in your Indian before we go, Tonty. He may have some news for us."

Tonty spoke to the sentinel, whose fingers visibly held the door, and he let pass a tall Iroquois brave carrying such a bundle of rich furs as one of that race above the condition of squaw rarely deigned to lift. His errand was evidently peaceable. He paused and stood like a prince. Neither La Salle nor Tonty remembered his face, though both felt sure he came from the mission village of friendly Iroquois near Fort Frontenac.

"What does my brother want?" inquired La Salle, with sympathy he never showed to his French subordinates.

"He waits to speak to his white brother with the iron hand," answered the Iroquois.

"Have you brought us bad news?" again inquired La Salle.

"Good news."

"What is it?"

"It is only to my brother with the iron hand."

"Can you not speak in the presence of Monsieur de la Salle?" demanded Tonty.

With exquisite reserve the Indian stood silent, waiting the conditions he needed for the delivery of his message.

"It is nothing which concerns me," said La Salle to Tonty. He prepared to stalk into the weather with Barbe.

Tonty spoke a few words to the waiting savage, who heard without returning any sign, and then followed Barbe, stretching the buffalo hide above her head. When La Salle observed this he failed to ridicule his lieutenant, but took one side of the shaggy canopy in his own hold. It was impossible for the girl to go dry-shod, but Tonty directed her way over the best and firmest ground. They made a solemn procession, for not a word was spoken. When they came to the fortress gate, Tonty again bestowed the robe around her as he had done when she entered the chapel, and stood bareheaded while Barbe—whispering "Adieu, monsieur"—passed out of his sight.

"I have thought of this, Tonty," said La Salle as he entered; "when she is a few years older she shall come to the fort on the Illinois, if I again reap success."

"Monsieur de la Salle, I am bound to tell you it will be dangerous for me ever to see mademoiselle again."

"Monsieur de Tonty," responded the explorer with his close smile, "I am bound to tell you I think it will be the safest imaginable arrangement for her."

The gate closed behind him, and Tonty carried back an exhilarated face to the waiting Iroquois.

He entered Father Hennepin's chapel again, and the Indian followed him to the hearth.

They stood there, ready for conference, the small black savage eye examining Tonty's face with open approval.

"Now let me have your message," said the Italian. "Have I ever seen you before? What is your name?"

"Sanomp," answered the Iroquois. "My white brother with the iron hand has not seen me before."

He spread open on the bench Barbe had occupied a present of fine furs and dried meat.

"Why does my brother bring me these things?" inquired Tonty, realizing as he looked at the gift how much of this barbarian's wealth was bestowed in such an offering.

"Listen," said Sanomp.[14] He had a face of benevolent gravity,—the unhurried, sincere face of man living close to Nature. "It is a chief of the Seneca tribe who speaks to my white brother."

"I have met a chief of the Seneca tribe before," remarked Tonty, smiling. "It was in the country of the Illinois, and he wrapped my scalp-lock around his fingers."

Sanomp smiled, too, without haste, and continued his story.

"I left my people to live near the fort of my French brothers because it was told me the man with a hand of iron was here. When I came here the man with a hand of iron was gone. So I waited for him. Our lives are consumed in waiting for the best things. Five years have I stood by the mouth of Cataraqui. And this morning the man with a hand of iron passed before my face."

He spoke a mixture of French and Iroquois which enabled Tonty to catch his entire meaning.

"But this hand could not betray me from the lake, to eyes that had never seen me before," objected the Italian.

Advancing one foot and folding his arms in the attitude of a narrator, the Indian said,—

"Listen. At that time of life when a young Iroquois retires from his tribe to hide in the woods and fast until his okie[15] is revealed to him, four days and four nights the boy Sanomp lay on the ground, rain and dew, moonlight and sunlight passing over him. The boy Sanomp looked up, for an eagle dropped before his eyes. He then knew that the eagle was his okie, and that he was to be a warrior, not a hunter or medicine-man. But the eagle dropped before the feet of a soldier the image of my white brother, and the soldier held up a hand of yellow metal. The boy heard a voice coming from the vision that said to him, 'Warrior, this is thy friend and brother. Be to him a friend and brother. After thou hast seven times followed the war path go and wait by the mouth of Cataraqui until he comes.' So when I had seven times followed the war path I came, and my brother being passed by, I waited."

Tonty's square brown Italian face was no more sincere than the redder aquiline visage fronting him and telling its vision.

"My brother Sanomp comes in a good time," he remarked.

The Iroquois next took out his peace pipe and pouch of tobacco. While he filled the bowl and stooped for an ember, Tonty stripped the copper hand of its glove. He held it up before Sanomp as he received the calumet in the other. An aboriginal grunt of strong satisfaction echoed in the chapel.

"Hand of yellow metal," said Sanomp.

Tonty gravely smoked the pipe and handed it back to Sanomp. Sanomp smoked it, shook the ashes out and put it away.

Thus was the ceremony of adoption finished. Without more talk, the red friend and brother turned from his white friend and brother and went back to his own world.

VIII.
TEGAHKOUITA.

Barbe ran breathless up the stairway, glad to catch sight of her uncle the Abbé so occupied at the lower hearth that he took no heed of her return.

She had counted herself the only woman in Fort Frontenac, yet she found a covered figure standing in front of the chamber door next her own.

Though Barbe had never seen Catharine Tegahkouita[16] she knew this must be the Iroquois virgin who lived a hermit life of devotion in a cabin at Lachine, revered by French and Indians alike. How this saint had reached Fort Frontenac or in whose behalf she was exerting herself Barbe could not conjecture. Tegahkouita had interceded for many afflicted people and her prayers were much sought after.

The Indian girl kept her face entirely covered. No man knew that it was comely or even what its features were like. The chronicler tells us when she was a young orphan beside her uncle's lodge-fire her eyes were too weak to bear the light of the sun, and in this darkness began the devotion which distinguished her life. What was first a necessity, became finally her choice, and she shut herself from the world.

To Barbe, Tegahkouita was an object of religious awe tempered by that criticism in which all young creatures secretly indulge. She sat on the bench as if in meditation, but her eyes crept up and down that straight and motionless and blanket-eclipsed presence. She knew that Tegahkouita was good; was it not told of the Indian girl that she rolled three days in a bed of thorns, and that she often walked barefooted in ice and snow, to discipline her body? She was not afraid of Tegahkouita. But she wished somebody else would come into the room who could break the saint's death-like silence. Sainthood was a very safe condition, but Barbe found it impossible to admire the outward appearance of a living saint.

La Salle had stopped at the barracks to order out his men, and Colin who had taken to that part of the fort for amusement, watched their transfer with much interest.

Wind was conquering rain. It blew keenly from the southwest, and sung at the corners of Frontenac, whirling dead leaves like fugitive birds into the area of the fort. La Salle's men turned out of their quarters with reluctance to exchange safety and comfort for exposure and a leaky camp. The explorer stood and saw them pass before him bearing their various burdens, excepting one man who slouched by the door of the bakehouse as if he had stationed himself there to see that they passed in order out of the gate.

"Come here, you Jolycœur," called La Salle, lifting his finger.

Jolycœur, savagely hairy, approached with that look of sulky menace La Salle never appeared to see in his servants.

"Where is your load of goods?" inquired the explorer.

"'Come here, you Jolycœur,' called La Salle."—*Page 138.*

Jolycœur lifted a quick look, and dropping itagain, replied, "Sieur de la Salle, I was waiting for the cook to hand me out the dishes you ordered against you came back."

La Salle examined him through half-shut eyes. It was this man's constant duty to prepare his food. Tonty and his brother Jean had so occupied his morning that he had found no time for eating. A man inured to hardships can fast with very little thought about the matter, but he decided if Jolycœur had not yet handled this meal he might hazard some last service from a man who had missed so many opportunities.

"Did you cook my breakfast?" he inquired.

"Sieur de la Salle, I dared not put my nose in the bakehouse. This cook is the worst man in Fort Frontenac."

The cook appearing with full hands in his door, La Salle said to Jolycœur, "Carry those platters into the lodge," and he watched the minutest action of the man's elbows, walking behind him into the lower apartment of the dwelling. A table stood there on which Jolycœur began to arrange the dishes with surly carelessness.

The explorer forgot him the moment they entered, for two people occupied this room in close talk. Challenging whatever ill Jacques le Ber and the Abbé Cavelier had prepared, La Salle advanced beyond the table with the chill and defiant bearing natural to him.

"Monsieur le Ber and I have been discussing this alliance you are so anxious to make with his family," spoke the Abbé.

The explorer met Le Ber's face full of that triumphant contempt which men strangely feel for other men who have fallen and become stepping-stones of fortune to themselves. He turned away without answer, and began to eat indifferently from the dishes Jolycœur had left ready, standing beside the table while he ate.

"If Jacques le Ber were as anxious for the marriage as yourself,—but I told you this morning, my brother La Salle, what madness it must seem to all sane men,—it could not be arranged. His daughter hath refused to see you."

"My thanks are due to my brother the Abbé for his nice management of all my affairs," sneered La Salle. "I comprehend there is nothing which he will not endeavor to mar for me. It surely is madness which induces a man against all experience to confide in his brother."

Jean Cavelier replied with a shrug and a spread of the hands which said, "In such coin of gratitude am I always paid."

"Sieur de la Salle," volunteered Le Ber, rising and coming forward with natural candor, "it is not so long ago that your proposal would have made me proud, and the Abbé hath not ill managed it now. Monsieur, I wish my girl to marry. I have been ready for any marriage she would accept. She has indeed shown more liking for you than for any other man in New France. Monsieur, I would far rather have her married than bound to the life she leads. But if you were in a position to marry, Jeanne refuses your hand."

"Has she said this to you?" inquired La Salle.

"I have not seen her to-day," replied Le Ber. "She has the Iroquois virgin Tegahkouita with her. I brought Tegahkouita here because she was besought for some healing in our Iroquois lodges near the fort."

Jacques le Ber stopped. But La Salle calmly heard him thus claim everything pertaining to Fort Frontenac.

"We must do what we can to hold these unstable Indians," continued Le Ber. "Monsieur, before I could carry your proposal to Jeanne, she sends me Tegahkouita, as if they had some holy contrivance for reading people's minds. Your brother will confirm to you the words Tegahkouita brought."

"Mademoiselle le Ber will pray for you always, my brother La Salle. But she refuses even to see you."

"It is easy enough for Jeanne to put you in her prayers," remarked the discontented father, "she hath room enough there for all New France."

The man who had more than once sprung into the midst of hostile savages and carried their admiration by a word, now stood silent and musing. But his face expressed nothing except determination.

"You shall see her yourself," Jacques le Ber exclaimed, with the shrewdness of a man holding present advantage, yet gauging fully his antagonist's force. "You and I were once friends, Sieur de la Salle. I might obtain a worse match for my girl."

"I will see her," said La Salle, more in the manner of affirming his own wish than of accepting a concession.

He mounted the stairs, with Le Ber behind him, the Abbé Cavelier following Le Ber.

As the father expected, Tegahkouita stood as a bar in front of Jeanne's chamber door. Slightly spreading her blanketed arms this Indian girl of peculiar gifts said slowly and melodiously in a voice tuned by much low-spoken prayer, "Mademoiselle Jeanne le Ber says, 'Tell Sieur de la Salle I will pray for him always, but I must never see his face again.'"

IX.
AN ORDEAL.

"When I have seen Mademoiselle le Ber," La Salle replied to the blanket of Tegahkouita, "I shall understand from herself what her wishes are in this matter."

"Sieur de la Salle cannot see her," spoke Tegahkouita. "She hath no word but this, and she will not see Sieur de la Salle again."

"I say he shall see her!" exclaimed the Montreal merchant, with asperity created by so many influences working upon his daughter. "He may look upon her this minute!"

Jeanne le Ber's presence in Fort Frontenac scarcely surprised Barbe, so great was her amazement at the attitude of her uncle La Salle. That he should be suing to Le Ber's daughter seemed as impossible as any rejection of his suit. She felt toward the saint she had pinched at convent that jealous resentment peculiar to women who desire to have the men of their families married, yet are never satisfied with the choice those men make. Even Barbe, however, considered it a sacrilegious act when Le Ber shook his daughter's door and demanded admittance.

Jeanne's complete silence, like a challenge, drew out his imperative force. He broke through every fastening and threw the door wide open.

The small, bare room, scarcely wider than its entrance, afforded no hiding-places. There was little to catch the eye, from rude berth to hooks in the ruder wall, from which the commandant's clothing had so lately been removed.

Jeanne, the focus of this small cell, had flown to its extremity. As the door burst from its fastenings, everybody in the outer room could see her standing against the wall with noble instinct, facing the breakers of her privacy, but without looking at them. Her eyes rested on her beads, which she told with rapid lips and fingers. A dormer window spread its background of light around her head.

The recoil of inaction which followed Le Ber's violence was not felt by Tegahkouita. With the swift silence of an Indian and the intuition of a devotee, she at once put herself in the sleeping cell, and kneeled holding up a crucifix before Jeanne. As this symbol of religion was lifted, Jeanne fell upon her knees.

Le Ber had not intended to enter, but indignation drove him on after Tegahkouita. He stood aside and did not approach his child,—a jealous, remorseful, anxious, irritated man.

La Salle could see Jeanne, though with giddy and indistinct vision. Her wool gown lay around her in carven folds, as she knelt like a victim ready for the headsman's axe.

One of the proudest and most reticent men who ever trod the soil of the New World was thus reduced to woo before his enemy and his kindred; to argue against those unseen forces represented by the Indian girl, and to fight death in his own body with every pleading respiration. For blindness was growing over his eyes. His lungs were tightened. When his back was turned in the room below, Jolycœur had mixed a dish for him.

La Salle's hardihood was the marvel of his followers. A body and will of electric strength carried him thousands of miles through ways called impassable. Defeat could not defeat him. But this struggle with Jeanne le Ber was harder than any struggle with an estranged king, harder than again bringing up fortune from the depths of ruin, harder than tearing his breath of life from the reluctant air. He reared himself against the chimney-side, pressing with palms and stretched fingers for support, yet maintaining a roused erectness.

"Jeanne!" he spoke; and eyes less blind than his could detect a sinking of her figure at the sound, "I have this to say."

With a plunging gait which terrified Barbe by its unnaturalness, La Salle attempted to place himself nearer the silent object he was to move. As he passed through the doorway he caught at the sides, and then stretched out and braced one palm against the wall. Thus propped he proceeded, articulating thickly but with careful exactness.

"Jeanne, when I have again brought success out of failure, I shall demand you in marriage. Your father permits it."

Her trembling lips prayed on, and she gave no token of having heard him, except the tremor which shook even the folds of her gown.

Too proud to confess his peril and make its appeal to her, and suppressing before so many witnesses her tender name of Sainte, he labored on as La Salle the explorer with the statement of his case.

"Perhaps I cannot see you again for some years. I do not ask words—of acceptance now. It is enough—if you look at me."

La Salle leaned forward. His eyeballs appeared to swell and protrude as he strained sight for the slightest lifting of the veil before that self-restraining spirit.

Barbe's wailing suddenly broke all bounds in the outer room. "My uncle the Abbé! Look at my uncle La Salle! He cannot breathe—he is going to die! Somebody has poisoned or stabbed my uncle La Salle!"

Jean Cavelier with lower outcry ran to help the explorer. But even a brother and a priest has his limitations. La Salle pushed him off.

When Barbe saw this, she threw herself to the floor and hid her face upon the bench. Her kinsman and the hero of her childhood was held over the abyss of death in the hand of Jeanne le Ber, while those who loved him must set their teeth in silence.

But neither this childish judge, nor the father watching for any slight motion of eyelids which might direct all his future hopes and plans, knew what sickening moisture started from every pore of Jeanne le Ber. Still she lifted her fainting eyes only as high as the crucifix Tegahkouita held before her. Compared to her duty as she saw it, she must count as nothing the life of the man she loved.

The Indian girl's weak sight had no plummet for the face of this greater devotee. Passionately white, its lips praying fast, it stared at the crucifix. Cold drops ran down from the dew which beaded temples and upper lip. Sieur de la Salle—Sieur de la Salle was dying, and asking her for a look! The lifting of her eyelids, the least wavering of her sight, would sweep away the vows she had made to Heaven, and loosen her soul for its swift rush to his breast. To be the wife of La Salle! Her mutter became almost audible as she slid the beads between her fingers. God would keep her from this deadly sin.

The gigantic will of La Salle, become almost material and visible, fell upon her with a cry which must have broken any other endurance.

"Jeanne! look at me now—you *shall* look at me now!"

Hoarse shouts of battle never tingled through blood as did the voice of this isolated man.

Jeanne's lips twitched on; she twisted her hands in tense knots against her neck, and her eyes maintained the level of the cross.

Silence—that fragment of eternity—then filled up the room, submerging strained ears. There were remote sounds, like the scream of wind cut by the angles of Fort Frontenac; but no sound which pierced the silence between La Salle and Jeanne le Ber.

He turned around and cast himself through the doorway with a lofty tread as if he were trying to mount skyward. The Abbé Cavelier extended both arms and kept him from stumbling over the settle which Barbe was baptizing with her anguish. She looked up with the distorted visage of one who weeps terribly, and saw the groping explorer led to the staircase. His feet plunged in the descent.

To this noise was added a distinct thud from Jeanne le Ber's room as her head struck the floor. She lay relaxed and prostrate, and her father lifted her up. Before rising to his feet with her he passed his hand piteously across her bruised forehead.

"She twisted her hands in tense knots against her neck."—*Page 152.*

X.
HEMLOCK.

Jolycœur, lounging with his shoulders against the barrack wall, gave furtive attention to La Salle as the explorer appeared within the fort. Even his eye was deceived by his master's bearing in giving him the signal to approach.

The wind was helpful to La Salle, but he only half met daylight and saw Jolycœur taking strange shapes.

"Go to Father Hennepin's old mission house," he slowly commanded, "and send Monsieur de Tonty directly to me."

The man, not daring to disobey until he could take refuge in Fort Frontenac with the gates closed behind the explorer, went on this errand.

"What ails Sieur de la Salle?" inquired the cook, coming out of his bakehouse to get this news of a sentinel.

They both watched the Abbé Cavelier making vain efforts to get hold of his misdirected brother.

"Gone mad with pride," suggested the sentinel. "The less he prospers the loftier I have always heard he bears himself. Would the governor of New France climb the wind with a tread like that?"

Outside the gate La Salle's limbs failed. The laboring Abbé then dragged him along, and it seemed an immense détour he was obliged to make to pass the extended foundation.

"Now you will believe my words which I spoke this morning concerning the peril we all stand in," panted this sorely taxed brother. "The Cavelier family is destroyed. My brother La Salle—Robert—my child! Shall I give you absolution?"

"Not yet," gasped La Salle.

"If you had ever taken my advice, this miserable end had not come upon you."

"I am not ended," gasped La Salle.

"Oh, my brother," lamented Jean Cavelier, tucking up his cassock as he bent to the strain, "I have but one consolation in my wretchedness. This is better for you than the marriage you would have made. What business have you to ally yourself with Le Ber? What business have you with marriage at all? For my part, I would object to any marriage you had in view, but Le Ber's daughter was the worst marriage for you in New France."

"Tonty!" gasped La Salle. With the swiftness of an Indian, Tonty was flying across the clearing. The explorer's unwary messenger Jolycœur he had left behind him bound with hide thongs and lying in Father Hennepin's inner room.

"Yes, yonder comes your Monsieur de Tonty who so easily gave up your post on the Illinois," panted the Abbé Cavelier. "Like all your worthless followers he hath no attachment to your person."

"There is more love in his iron hand," La Salle's paralyzing mouth flung out, "than in any other living heart!"

Needing no explanation from the Abbé, the commandant from Fort St. Louis took strong hold of La Salle and hurried him to the mission house. They faced the wind, and Tonty's cap blew off, his rings of black hair flaring to a fierce uprightness.

The surgeon ran out of the dwelling and met and helped them in, and thus tardily resistance to the poison was begun, but it had found its hardiest victim since the day of Socrates.

Tonty's iron hand brought out of Jolycœur immediate confession of the poison he had used.

In an age when most cunning and deadly drugs were freely handled, and men who would not shed blood thought it no sin to take enemies neatly off the scene by the magic of a dish, Jolycœur was not without knowledge of a plant called hemlock, growing ready to the hand of a good poisoner in the New World.

Noon stood in the sky, half shredding vapors, and lighting cool sparkles upon the lake. Afternoon dragged its mute and heavy hours westward.

Men left the mission house and entered it again, carrying wood or water.

"His rings of black hair flaring to a fierce uprightness."—*Page 158.*

The sun set in the lake, parting clouds before his sinking visage and stretching his rays like long arms of fire to smite the heaving water.

Twilight rose out of the earth and crept skyward, blotting all visible shore. Fort Frontenac stood an indistinct mass beside the Cataraqui, as beside another lake. Stars seemed to run and meet and dive in long ripples. The wash of water up the sand subsided in force as the wind sunk, leaving air space for that ceaseless tune breathed by a great forest.

Overhead, from a port of cloud, the moon's sail pushed out suddenly, less round than it had been the night before, and owning by such depression that she had begun tacking toward her third quarter. Fort and settlements again found their proportions, and Father Hennepin's cross stood clear and fair, throwing its shadow across the mission house.

Within the silent mission house warmth and redness were diffused from logs piled in the chimney.

The Abbé Cavelier's cassock rose and fell with that sleep which follows great anxiety and exhaustion. He reclined against the lowest step of a broken ladder-way which once ascended from corner to loft. The men, except one who stood guard outside in the shadow of the house, were asleep in the next room.

La Salle rested before the hearth on some of the skins Tonty had received from his Indian friend and brother. Whenever the explorer opened his eyes he saw Tonty sitting awake on the floor beside him.

"Sleep," urged La Salle.

"I shall not sleep again," said Tonty, "until I see you safely on your way toward France."

"This has been worse than the dose of verdigris I once got."

"Jolycœur says he used hemlock," responded Tonty. "He accused everybody in New France of setting him on to the deed, but I silenced that."

"I had not yet dismissed him, Tonty. The scoundrel hath claims on me for two years' wages."

"He should have got his wages of me," exclaimed Tonty, "if this proved your death. He should have as many bullets as his body could hold."

"Tonty, untie the fellow and turn him out and discharge his wages for me with some of the skins you have put under me." La Salle rose on his elbow and then sat up. His face was very haggard, but the practical clear eye dominated it. "These fellows cannot balk me. I have lost all that makes life, except my friend. But I shall come back and take the great west yet! A man with a purpose cannot be killed, Tonty. He goes on. He must go on."

BOOK III.
FORT ST. LOUIS OF THE ILLINOIS.
1687 A. D.

I.
IN AN EAGLE'S NEST.

"Fort Lewis is in the country of the Illinois and seated on a steep Rock about two hundred Foot high, the River running at the Bottom of it. It is only fortified with Stakes and Palisades, and some Houses advancing to the Edge of the Rock. It has a very spacious Esplanade, or Place of Arms. The Place is naturally strong, and might be made so by Art, with little expence. Several of the Natives live in it, in their Huts. I cannot give an Account of the Latitude it stands in, for want of proper Instruments to take an Observation, but Nothing can be pleasanter; and it may be truly affirmed that the Country of the Illinois enjoys all that can make it accomplished, not only as to Ornament, but also for its plentiful Production of all Things requisite for the Support of human Life.

"The Plain, which is watered by the River, is beautified by two small Hills about half a League distant from the Fort, and those Hills are cover'd with groves of Oaks, Walnut-Trees, and other Sorts I have named elsewhere. The Fields are full of Grass, growing up very high. On the Sides of the Hills is found a gravelly Sort of Stone, very fit to make Lime for Building. There are also many Clay Pits, fit for making of Earthen Ware, Bricks, and Tiles, and along the River there are Coal Pits, the Coal whereof has been try'd and found very good."[17]

The young man lifted his pen from the paper and stood up beside a box in the storehouse which had served him as table, at the demand of a priestly voice.

"Joutel, what are you writing there?"

"Monsieur the Abbé, I was merely setting down a few words about this Fort St. Louis of the Illinois in which we are sheltered. But my candle is so nearly burned out I will put the leaves aside."

"You were writing nothing else?" insisted La Salle's brother, setting his shoulders against the storehouse door.

"Not a word, monsieur."

The Abbé's ragged cassock scarcely showed such wear as his face, which the years that had handled him could by no means have cut into such deep grooves or moulded into such ghastly hillocks of features.

"I cannot sleep to-night, Joutel," said the Abbé Cavelier.

"I thought you were made very comfortable in the house," remarked Joutel.

"What can make me comfortable now?"

They stood still, saying nothing, while a candle waved its feeble plume with uncertainty over its marsh of tallow, making their huge shadows stagger over log-wall or floor or across piled merchandise. One side of the room was filled with stacked buffalo hides, on which Joutel, nightly, took the complete rest he had earned by long tramping in southern woods.

He rested his knuckles on the box and looked down. A Norman follower of the Caveliers, he had done La Salle good service, but between the Abbé and him lay a reason for silence.

"Joutel, what are you writing there?"—*Page 169.*

"Tonty may reach the Rock at any time,"[18] complained the Abbé to the floor, though his voice must reach Joutel's ears. "There is nothing I dread more than meeting Tonty."

"We can leave the Rock before Monsieur de Tonty arrives," said Joutel, repeating a suggestion he had made many times.

"Certainly, without the goods my brother would have him deliver to me, without a canoe or any provision whatever for our journey!"

"They say here that Monsieur de Tonty led only two hundred Indians and fifty Frenchmen to aid the new governor in his war against the Iroquois," observed Joutel. "He may not come back at all."

"I have thought of that," the Abbé mused. "If Tonty be dead we are indeed wasting our time here, when we ought to be well on our way to Quebec, to say naught of the voyage to France. But this fellow in charge of the Rock refuses to honor my demands without more authority."

"He received us most kindly, and we have been his guests a month," said Joutel.

"I would be his guest no longer than this passing night if my difficulties were solved," said the Abbé. "For there is even Colin's sister to torment me. I know not where she is,—whether in Montreal or in the wilderness between Montreal and this fort. If I had taken her back with Colin to France, she would now be safe with my mother. There was another evidence of my poor brother's madness! He was determined Mademoiselle Cavelier should be sent out to Fort St. Louis. When he sailed on that last great voyage, he sat in one of the ships the king furnished him and in the last lines he wrote his mother refused to tell her his destination! And at the same time he wrote instructions to the nuns of St. Joseph concerning the niece whose guardian he never was. She must be sent to Fort St. Louis at the first safe opportunity! She was to have a grant in this country to replace her fortune which he had used. And this he only told me during his fever at St. Domingo on the voyage."

Joutel folded and put away his notes. The Abbé's often repeated complaints seldom stirred a reply from him. Though on this occasion he thought of saying,—

"Monsieur de Tonty may bring news of her from Montreal."

"You understand, Joutel," exclaimed the Abbé, approaching the candle, "that it is best,—that it is necessary not to tell Tonty what we know?"

"I have understood what you said, Monsieur the Abbé."

"You are the only man who gives me anxiety. All the rest are willing to keep silence. Is it not my affair? I wish you would cease writing your scraps. It irritates me to come into this storehouse and find you writing your scraps." He looked severely at the young man, who leaned against the box making no further promise or reply. Then seizing the candle, the Abbé stepped to a bed made of bales, where, wrapped in skins and blankets, young Colin Cavelier lay uttering the acknowledgement of peaceful sleep. Another boy lay similarly wrapped on the floor beside him.

The priest's look at these two was brief. He went on to the remaining man in the room, a hairy fellow, lying coiled among hides and pressed quite into a corner. The man appeared unconscious, emitting his breath in short puffs.

Abbé Cavelier gazed upon him with shudders.

The over-taxed candle flame stooped and expired, the scent of its funeral pile rising from a small red point in darkness.

II.
THE FRIEND AND BROTHER

While Abbé Cavelier stood in the storehouse, Tonty, a few miles away, was setting his camp around a spring of sulphur water well known to the hunters of St. Louis. The spring boiled its white sand from unmeasured depths at the root of an oak, and spread a pool which slipped over its barrier in a thin stream to the Illinois.

Though so near his fortress, Tonty and Greysolon du Lhut, fresh from their victorious campaign with the governor of New France against the Iroquois, thought it not best to expose their long array of canoes in darkness on the river. They had with them[19] women and children,— fragments of families, going under their escort to join the colony at Fort St. Louis.

Du Lhut's army of Indians from the upper lakes had returned directly to their own villages to celebrate the victory; but that unwearied rover himself, with a few followers, had dragged his gouty limbs across portages to the Illinois, to sojourn longer with Tonty.

Their camp was some distance from the river, up an alluvial slope of the north shore. Opposite, a line of cliffs, against which the Illinois washes for miles, caught the eye through darkness by its sandy glint; and not far away, on the north side of the river, that long ridge known as Buffalo Rock made a mass of gloom.

Dependent and unarmed colonists were placed in the centre of the camp. Tonty himself, with his usual care on this journey, had helped to pitch a tent of blankets and freshly cut poles for Mademoiselle Barbe Cavelier and the officer's wife, who clung to her in the character of guardian. The other immigrants understood and took pleasure in this small temporary home, built nightly for a girl whose proud silence among them they forgave as the caprice of beauty. The wife of the officer Bellefontaine, on her part, rewarded Tonty by attaching her ceaseless presence to Barbe. She was a timid woman, very small-eyed and silent, who took refuge in Barbe's larger shadow, and found it convenient for an under-sized duenna whose husband was so far in the wilds.

Mademoiselle Cavelier was going to Fort St. Louis at the first opportunity since her uncle La Salle's request, made three years before.

At this time it was not known whether La Salle had succeeded or failed in his last enterprise. He had again convinced the king. His seigniories and forts were restored to him, and governor's agents and associates driven out of his possessions. He had sailed from France with a fleet of ships, carrying a large colony to plant at the Mississippi's mouth. His brother the Abbé Cavelier, two nephews, priests, artisans, young men, and families were in his company, which altogether numbered over four hundred people.

Fogs or storms, or dogged navigators disagreeing with and disobeying him, had robbed him of his destination; for news came back to France, by a returning ship, of loss and disaster and a colony dropped like castaways on some inlet of the Gulf.

The evening meal was eaten and sentinels were posted. Even petulant children had ceased to fret within the various enclosures. Indians and Frenchmen lay asleep under their canoes which they had carried from the river, and by propping with stones or stakes at one side, converted into low-roofed shelters.

Barbe's tent was beside the spring near the camp-fire. She could, by parting overlapped blanket edges, look out of her cloth house into those living depths of bubbling white sand, so like the thoughts of young maids. Two or three fallen leaves, curled into quaint craft, slid across the pool's surface, hung at its barrier, and one after the other slipped over and disappeared along the thread of water. A hollow of light was scooped above the camp-fire, outside of which darkness stood an impenetrable rind, for the sky had all day been thickened by clouds.

The Demoiselle Bellefontaine, tucked neatly as a mole under her ridge, rested from her fears in sleep; and Barbe made ready to lie down also, sweeping once more the visible world with a lingering eye. She saw an Indian creeping on hands and knees toward Tonty's lodge. He entered darkness the moment she saw him. The girl arose trembling and put on her clothes. She had caught no impression of his tribe; but if he were a warrior of the camp, his crawling so secretly must threaten harm to Tonty. She did not distinctly know what she ought to do, except warn Monsieur de Tonty.

But on a sudden the iron-handed commandant ran past her tent, shouting to his men. There was a sound like the rushing of bees through the air, and horrible faces smeared with paint, tattooed bodies, and hands brandishing weapons closed in from darkness; the men of the camp rose up with answering yells, and the flash and roar of muskets surrounded Barbe as if she were standing in some nightmare world of lightning and thunder. She heard the screams of children and frightened mothers. She saw Tonty in meteor rushes rallying men, and striking down, with nothing but his iron hand, a foe who had come to quarters too close for fire-arms. Indian after Indian fell under that sledge, and a cry of terror in Iroquois French, which she could understand, rose through the whoop of invasion,—

"The Great-Medicine-Hand! The Great-Medicine-Hand!"

Brands were caught from the fire and thrown like bolts, sparks hissing as they flew. Her tent was overturned and she fell under it with the Demoiselle Bellefontaine, who uttered muffled squeals.

When Barbe dragged her companion out of the midst of poles, all the hurricane of action had passed by. Its rush could be heard down the slope, then the splashing of bodies and tumultuous paddling in the river. Guns yet flashed. She heard Frenchmen and Illinois running with their canoes down to the water to give chase. Farther and farther away sounded the retreat, and though women and children continued to make outcry, Barbe could hear no groans.

The brands of the fire were still scattered, but hands were busy collecting and bringing them back,—processions of gigantic glow-worms meeting by dumb appointment in a nest of hot ashes and trodden logs. All faces were drowned in the dark until these re-united embers fitfully brought them out. A crowd of frightened immigrants drew around the blaze, calling each other by name, and demanding to know who was scalped.

Barbe saw nothing better to do than to stand beside her wrecked tent, and the Demoiselle Bellefontaine burrowed closely to her, uttering distressed noises.

The pursuers presently returned and quieted the camp. Tonty had not lost a man, though a few were wounded. The attacking party carried off with them every trace of their repulse.

Overturned lodges were now set straight, and as soon as Bellefontaine's wife found hers inhabitable she hid herself within it. But Barbe waited to ask the busy commandant,—

"Monsieur de Tonty, have you any wound?"

"No, mademoiselle," he answered, pausing to breathe himself, and seize upon an interview so unusual. "I hope you have not been greatly disturbed. The Iroquois are now entirely driven off, and they will not venture to attack us again."

With excited voice Barbe assured him she had remained tranquil through the battle.

"We do not call this a battle," laughed Tonty. "These were a party of Senecas, who rallied after defeat and have followed us to our own country. They tried to take the camp by surprise, and nearly did it; but Sanomp crept between sentinels and waked me."

"Who is Sanomp, monsieur?"

"Do you remember the Iroquois Indian who came to Father Hennepin's chapel at Fort Frontenac?"

"Yes, monsieur; was he among these Senecas?"

"The Senecas are his tribe of the Iroquois, mademoiselle. He was among them; but he has left his people for my sake. These Indians have visions and obey them. He said the time had come for him to follow me."

"Sanomp was then the Indian I saw creeping toward your tent. Did he fight against his own people?"

"No, mademoiselle. While Du Lhut and I flew to rouse the camp, he sat doggedly down where he found me. This was a last chance for the Senecas. We are so near Fort St. Louis, and almost within shouting distance of our Miamis on Buffalo Rock. Such security makes sentinels careless. Sanomp crept ahead of the others and whispered in my ear, taking his chance of being brained before I understood him. He has proved himself my friend and brother, mademoiselle, to do this for me, and moreover to bear the shame of sitting crouched like a squaw through a fray."

"Everybody loves and fears Monsieur de Tonty,"[20] observed Barbe, with sedate accent.

Tonty breathed deeply.

"Am I an object of fear to you, mademoiselle? Doubtless I have grown like a buffalo," he ruminated. "Perhaps you feel a natural aversion toward a man bearing a hand of iron."

"On the contrary, it seemed a great convenience among the Indians," murmured Barbe, and Tonty laughed and stood silent.

The camp was again settling to rest, and fewer swarming figures peopled the darkness. Winding and aspiring through new fuel the camp-fire once more began to lift its impalpable pavilion, and groups sat around it beneath that canopy of tremulous light, with rapid talk and gesture repeating to each other their impressions of the Senecas' attack."Mademoiselle," said Tonty, lifting his left hand to his bare head, for he had rushed hatless into action, "good-night. The guards are doubled. You are more secure than when you lay down before.""Good-night, monsieur," replied Barbe, and he opened her tent for her, when she turned back."Monsieur de Tonty," she whispered swiftly, "I have had no chance during this long journey,—for with you alone would I speak of it,—to demand if you believe that saying against yourself which they are wickedly charging to my uncle La Salle?"

"Mademoiselle, how could I believe that Monsieur de la Salle said in France he wished to be rid of me? One laughs at a rumor like that."

"The tales lately told about his madness are more than I can bear."

"Mademoiselle, Monsieur de la Salle's enemies always called his great enterprises madness."

"Can you imagine where he now is, Monsieur de Tonty?"

"Oh, heavens!" Tonty groaned. "Often have I said to myself,—Has Monsieur de la Salle been two years in America, and I have not joined him, or even spoken with him? It is not my fault! As soon as I believed he had reached the Gulf of Mexico I descended the Mississippi. I searched all those countries, every cape and every shore. I demanded of all the natives where he was, and not one could tell me a word. Judge of my pain and my dolor."[21]

They stood in such silence as could result from two people's ceasing to murmur in the midst of high-pitched voices.

"Monsieur de Tonty," resumed Barbe, "do you remember Jeanne le Ber?"

"Mademoiselle, I never saw her."

"She refused my uncle La Salle at Fort Frontenac, and I detested her for it. In the new church at Montreal she has had a cell made behind the altar. There she prays day and night. She wears only a blanket, but the nun who feeds her says her face is like an angel's. Monsieur, Jeanne le Ber fell with her head bumping the floor,—and I understood her. She had a spirit fit to match with my uncle La Salle's. She thought she was right. I forgave her then, for I know, monsieur, she loved my uncle La Salle."

When Barbe had spoken such daring words she stepped inside her tent and dropped its curtain.

III.
HALF-SILENCE.

The October of the Mississippi valley—full of mild nights and mellow days and the shine of ripened corn—next morning floated all the region around Fort St. Louis in silver vapor. The two small cannon on the Rock began to roar salutes as soon as Tonty's line of canoes appeared moving down the river.

To Barbe this was an enchanted land. She sat by the Demoiselle Bellefontaine and watched its populous beauty unfold. Blue lodge-smoke arose everywhere. Tonty pointed out the Shawnee settlement eastward, and the great town of the Illinois northwest of the Rock,—a city of high lodges shaped like the top of a modern emigrant wagon. He told where Piankishaws and Weas might be distinguished, how many Shawanoes were settled beyond the ravine back of the Rock, and how many thousand people, altogether, were collected in this principality of Monsieur de la Salle.

A castellated cliff with turrets of glittering sandstone towered above the boats, but beyond that,—round, bold, and isolated, its rugged breasts decked with green, its base washed by the river,—the Rock[22] of St. Louis waited whatever might be coming in its eternal leisure. Frenchmen and Indians leaped upon earthworks at its top and waved a welcome side by side, the flag of France flying above their heads.

At Barbe's right hand lay an alluvial valley bordered by a ridge of hills a mile away. Along this ancient river-bed Indian women left off gathering maize from standing stalks, and ran joyfully crying out to receive their victorious warriors. Inmates poured from the settlement of French cabins opposite and around the Rock. With cannon booming overhead, Tonty passed its base followed by the people who were to ascend with him, and landed west of it, on a sandy strip where the voyager could lay his hand on that rugged fern-tufted foundation. Barbe and the Demoiselle Bellefontaine followed him along a path cut through thickets, around moss-softened irregular heights of sandstone, girdled in below and bulging out above, so that no man could obtain foothold to scale them. Gnarled tree-roots, like folds of snakes caught between closing strata, hung, writhed in and out. The path, under pine needles and fallen leaves, was cushioned with sand white as powdered snow. Behind the Rock, stretching toward a ravine, were expanses of this lily sand which looked fresh from the hands of the Maker, as if even a raindrop had never indented its whiteness.

Three or four foot-holes were cut in the southeast flank of rock wall. An Indian ran down from above and flung a rope over to Tonty. He mounted these rocky stirrups first, helped by the rope, and knelt to reach back for Barbe and the Demoiselle Bellefontaine. The next ascent was up water-terraced rock to an angle as high as their waists. Here two more stirrups were cut in the rock. Ferns brushed their faces, and shrubs stooped over them. The heights were studded thick with gigantic trees half-stripped of leaves. Rust-colored lichens and lichens hoary like blanched old men, spread their great seals on stone and soil.

Wide water-terraced steps, looking as if cut for a temple, ascended at last to the gate. Through this Tonty led his charge upon a dimpled sward, for care had been taken to keep turf alive in Fort St. Louis.

Recognition and joy were the first sensations of many immigrants entering, as the people they loved received them. But Barbe felt only delicious freedom in such a crag castle. There was a sound of the sea in pine trees all around. The top of the Rock was nearly an acre in extent. It was fortified by earthworks, except the cliff above the river, which was set with palisades and the principal dwellings of the fort. There were besides, a storehouse, a block-house, and several Indian lodges. But the whole space—so shaded yet so sunny, reared high in air yet sheltered as a nest—was itself such a temple of security that any buildings within it seemed an impertinence. The centre, bearing its flagstaff, was left open.

Two priests, a Récollet and a Sulpitian, met Tonty and the girl he led in, the Sulpitian receiving her in his arms and bestowing a kiss on her forehead.

"Oh, my uncle Abbé!" Barbe gasped with surprise. "Is Colin with you? Is my uncle La Salle here?"

But Tonty, swifter than the Abbé's reply, laid hold of the Récollet Father and drew him beside Abbé Cavelier, demanding without greeting or pause for courteous compliment,—

"Is Monsieur de la Salle safe and well? You both come from Monsieur de la Salle!"

"He was well when we parted from him," replied the Abbé Cavelier, looking at a bunch of maiden-hair fern which Barbe had caught from a ledge and tucked in the bosom of her gown. "We left him on the north branch of the Trinity River, Monsieur de Tonty."

The Récollet said nothing, but kept his eyes fixed on his folded hands. Tonty, too eager to mark well both bearers of such news, demanded again impartially,—

"And he was well?"

"He left us in excellent health, monsieur."

"How glad I am to find you in Fort St. Louis!" exclaimed Tonty. "This is the first direct message I have had from Monsieur de la Salle since he sailed from France. How many men are in your party? Have you been made comfortable?"

"Only six, monsieur. We have been made quite comfortable by your officer Bellefontaine."

"**And he was well?**"—*Page 192.*

"Monsieur the Abbé, where did Monsieur de la Salle land his colony?"

"On a western coast of the Gulf, monsieur. It was most unfortunate. Ever since he has been searching for the Mississippi."

"While I searched for him. Oh, Fathers!" Tonty's voice deepened and his swarthy joyful face set its contrast opposite two downcast churchmen, "nothing in Fort St. Louis is good enough for messengers from Monsieur de la Salle. What can I do for you? Did he send me no orders?"

"He did commit a paper to my hand, naming skins and merchandise that he would have delivered to me, as well as a canoe and provisions for our journey to New France."

"Come, let me see this paper," demanded Tonty. "Whatever Monsieur de la Salle orders shall be done at once; but the season is now so advanced you will not push on to New France until spring."

"That is the very reason, Monsieur de Tonty, why we should push on at once. We have waited a month for your return. I leave Fort St. Louis with my party to-morrow, if you will so forward my wishes."

"Monsieur the Abbé, it is impossible! You have yet told me nothing of all it is necessary for me to know touching Monsieur de la Salle."

"To-morrow," repeated the Abbé Cavelier, "I must set out at dawn, if you can honor my brother's paper."

Tonty, with a gesture of his left hand, led the way to his quarters across the esplanade. As Barbe walked behind the Récollet Father, she wondered why he had given no answer to any of Tonty's questions.

Her brother advanced to meet her, and she ran and gave him her hands and her cheek to kiss. They had been apart four years, and looked at each other with scrutinizing gaze. He overtopped her by a head. Barbe expected to find him tall and rudely masculine, but there was change in him for which she was not prepared.

"My sister has grown charming," pronounced Colin. "Not as large as the Caveliers usually are, but like a bird exquisite in make and graceful motion."

"Oh, Colin, what is the matter?" demanded Barbe, with direct dart. "I see concealment in your face!"

"What do you see concealed? Perhaps you will tell me that." He became mottled with those red and white spots which are the blood's protest against the will.

"The Récollet Father did not answer a word to Monsieur de Tonty's questions, Colin; and the voice of my uncle the Abbé sounded unnatural. Is there wicked power in those countries you have visited to make you all come back like men half asleep from some drug?"

"Yes, there is!" exclaimed the boy; "I hate that wilderness. When we are once in France I will never venture into such wilds again. They dull me until my tongue seems dead."

"And, Colin, you did leave my uncle La Salle quite well?"

"It was he who left us. He was in excellent health the last time we saw him." The boy spoke these words with precision, and Barbe sighed her relief.

"For myself," she said, "I love this wild world. I shall stay here until my uncle La Salle arrives."

"Our uncle the Abbé will decide that," replied Colin. "It is unfortunate that you left Montreal. Your only hope of staying here rests on the hard journey before us, and the risks we run of meeting winter on the way. I wish you had been sent to France. I wish we were all in France now." Colin's face relaxed wistfully.

Two crows were scolding in the trees below them. Barbe felt ready to weep; as if the tender spirit of autumn had stolen through her, as mists steal along the hills. She sat down on the grassy earthwork, and Colin picked some pine needles from a branch and stood silent beside her, chewing them.

But those vague moods which haunt girlhood held always short dominion over Barbe. She was in close kinship with the world around, and the life of the fort began to occupy her.

The Rock was like a small fair with its additional inhabitants, who were still running about in a confusion of joyful noises. Children, delighted to be freed from canoes at so bright a time of day, raced across the centre, or hid behind wigwam or tree, calling to each other. An Indian stalked across to the front of the Rock, and Barbe watched him reach out through an opening in the low log palisade. A platform was there built on the trunks of two leaning cedars. The Indian unwound a windlass and let down a bucket to the river below. She heard its distant splash and some of its resounding drips on the way up. Living in Fort St. Louis was certainly like living on a cloud.

"I will go into the officers' house," suggested Colin, "and see how the Abbé's demands are met by Monsieur de Tonty. We shall then know if we are to set out for Quebec to-morrow."

IV.
A FÊTE ON THE ROCK.

Barbe did not object or assent. Youth shoves off any evil day by ignoring it, and Colin left her in lazy enjoyment of the populous place.

The Demoiselle Bellefontaine approached to ask if she desired to come to the apartment the commandant reserved for her; but Barbe replied that she wished to sit there and amuse herself awhile longer with the novelty of Fort St. Louis.

A child she had noticed on the journey brought her, as great treasure, a handful of flints and crumble-dust from the sandstone. They sorted the stuff on her knee,—fat-faced dark French child and young girl fine enough to be the sylvan spirit of the Rock.

Mademoiselle Cavelier's wardrobe was by no means equal to that gorgeous period in which she lived, being planned by her uncle the Abbé and executed by the frugal and exact hands of a self-denying sisterhood. But who can hide a girl's supple slimness in a gown plain as a nun's, or take the blossom-burnish off her face with colonial caps? Dark curls showed around her temples. Barbe's aquiline face had received scarcely a mark since Tonty saw it at Fort Frontenac. The gentle monotonous restraint of convent life had calmed her wild impulses, and she was in that trance of expecting great things to come, which is the beautiful birthright of youth.

While she was sorting arrow-head chips, her uncle came out of Tonty's quarters and cast his eye about the open space in search of her. At his approach Barbe's playmate slipped away, and the Abbé placed himself in front of her with his hands behind him.

Barbe gave him a scanty look, feeling sure he came to announce the next day's journey. This man, having many excellences, yet roused constant antagonism in his brother and the niece most like that brother. When he protruded his lower lip and looked determined, Barbe thought if the sin could be set aside a plunge in the river would be better than this journey.

"I have a proposal for you, my child," said the Abbé. "It comes from Monsieur de Tonty. He tells me my brother La Salle encouraged him to hope for this alliance, and I must declare I see no other object my brother La Salle had in view when he sent you to Fort St. Louis. Monsieur de Tonty understands the state of your fortune. On his part, he holds this seigniory jointly with my brother, and the traffic he is able to control brings no mean revenue. It is true he lacks a hand. But it hath been well replaced by the artificer, and he comes of an Italian family of rank."

Barbe's head was turned so entirely away that the mere back of a scarlet ear was left to the Abbé. One hand clutched her lap and the other pulled grass with destructive fingers.

"Having stated Monsieur de Tonty's case I will now state mine," proceeded her uncle. "I leave this fort before to-morrow dawn. I must take you with me or leave you here a bride. The journey is perilous for a small party and we may not reach France until next year. And an alliance like this will hardly be found in France for a girl of uncertain fortune. Therefore I have betrothed you to Monsieur de Tonty, and you will be married this evening at vespers."

"You have stated Monsieur de Tonty's case, and you have stated yours," said Barbe. "I will now state mine. I will not be married to any man at a day's notice."

"May I ask what it is you demand, mademoiselle?" inquired the Abbé, with irony, "if you propose to re-arrange any marriage your relatives make for you."

"I demand a week between the betrothal and the marriage."

"A week, mademoiselle!" her uncle laughed. "We who set out must give winter a week's start of us for such a whim! You will be married to-night or you will return with me to France. I will now send Monsieur de Tonty to you to be received as your future husband."

"I will scratch him!" exclaimed Barbe, with a flash of perverseness, at which her uncle's cassocked shoulders shook until he disappeared within doors.

She left the earthwork and went to the entrance side of the fort. There she stood, whispering with a frown,—"Oh, if you please, monsieur, keep your distance! Do not come here as any future husband of mine!"

She had, however, much time in which to prepare her mind before Tonty appeared.

All eyes on the Rock followed him. He shone through the trees, a splendid figure in the gold and white uniform of France, laid aside for years but resumed on this great occasion.

When he came up to Barbe he stopped and folded his arms, saying whimsically,—

"Mademoiselle, I have not the experience to know how one should approach his betrothed. I never was married before."

"It is my case, also, monsieur," replied Barbe.

"How do you like Fort St. Louis?" proceeded Tonty.

"I am enchanted with it."

"You delight me when you say that. During the last four years I have not made an improvement about the land or in any way strengthened this position without thinking, Mademoiselle Cavelier may sometime approve of this. We are finding a new way of heating our houses with underground flues made of stone and mortar."

"That must be agreeable, monsieur."

"We often have hunting parties from the Rock. This country is full of game."

"It is pleasant to amuse one's self, monsieur."

Tonty had many a time seen the silent courtship of the Illinois. He thought now of those motionless figures sitting side by side under a shelter of rushes or bark from morning till night without exchanging a word.

"Mademoiselle, I hope this marriage is agreeable to you?"

"Monsieur de Tonty," exclaimed Barbe, "I have simply been flung at your head to suit the convenience of my relatives."

"Was that distasteful to you?" he wistfully inquired.

"I am not fit for a bride. No preparation has been made for me."

"I thought of making some preparation myself," confessed Tonty. "I got a web of brocaded silk from France several years ago."

"To be clothed like a princess by one's bridegroom," said Barbe, wringing her gown skirt and twisting folds of it in her fingers. "That might be submitted to. But I could not wear the web of brocade around me like a blanket."

"There are fifty needlewomen on the Rock who can make it in a day, mademoiselle."

"And in short, monsieur, to be betrothed in the morning and married the same day is what no girl will submit to!"

Tonty, in the prime of his manhood and his might as a lover was too imposing a figure for her to face; she missed seeing his swarthy pallor as he answered,—

"I understand from all this, mademoiselle, that you care nothing for me. I have felt betrothed to you ever since I declared myself to Monsieur de la Salle at Fort Frontenac. How your pretty dreaming of the Rock of St. Louis and your homesick cry for this place did pierce me! I said, 'She shall be my wife, and I will bring home everything that can be obtained for her. That small face shall be heart's treasure to me. Its eyes will watch for me over the Rock.' On our journey here, many a night I took my blanket and lay beside your tent, thanking the saints for the sweet privilege of bringing home my bride. Mademoiselle," said Tonty, trembling, "I will kill any other man who dares approach you. Yet, mademoiselle, I could not annoy you by the least grief! Oh, teach a frontiersman what to say to please a woman!"

"Monsieur de Tonty," panted Barbe. "You please me too well, indeed! It was necessary to come to an understanding. You should not make me say,—for I am ashamed to tell,—how long I have adored you!"

As Tonty's quick Italian blood mounted from extreme anguish to extreme rapture, he laughed with a sob.

Fifty needlewomen on the Rock made in a day a gown of the web of brocaded silk. The fortress was full of preparation for evening festivity. Hunters went out and brought in game, and Indians carried up fish, new corn, and honey from wild bee trees. All the tables which the dwellings afforded were ranged in two rows at opposite sides of the place of arms, and decorated with festoons of ferns and cedar, and such late flowers as exploring children could find.

Some urchins ascended the Rock with an offering of thick-lobed prickly cactus which grew plentifully in the sand. The Demoiselle Bellefontaine labored from place to place, helping her husband to make this the most celebrated fête ever attempted in Fort St. Louis.

As twilight settled—and it slowly settled—on the summit, roast venison, buffalo steaks, and the odor of innumerable dishes scented the air. Many candles pinned to the branches of trees like vast candelabra, glittered through the dusk. Crows sat on the rocks below and gabbled of the corn they had that day stolen from lazy Indian women.

There was no need of chapel or bell in a temple fortress. All the inhabitants of the Rock stood as witnesses. Colin brought Barbe from the dwelling with the greater part of the web of brocaded silk dragged in grandeur behind her. Tonty kissed her hand and led her before the priests. When the ceremony ended a salute was fired.

The Illinois town could hear singing on the Rock and see that stronghold glittering as if it had been carried by torches. Music of violin and horn, laughter, dancing, and gay voices in repartee sounded on there through half the hours of the night.

V.
THE UNDESPAIRING NORMAN.

The morning star yet shone and the river valley was drenched with half frosty dew, and filled with silver mist when the Abbé Cavelier and his party descended to their canoes and set off up the river. They had made their farewells the night before, but Tonty and Greysolon du Lhut appeared, Tonty accompanying them down the descent. He came up with a bound before the boat was off, thundered at Bellefontaine's door, and pulled that sleepy officer into the open air, calling at his ear,—

"What fellow is this in the Abbé's party who kept out of my sight until he carried his load but now to the canoe?"

"You must mean Teissier, Monsieur de Tonty. He has lain ailing in the storehouse."

"Look,—yonder he goes."

Tonty made Bellefontaine lean over the eastern earthwork, but even the boat was blurred upon the river.

"That was Jolycœur," declared Tonty, "whom Monsieur de la Salle promised me he would never take into his service again. That fellow tried to poison Monsieur de la Salle at Fort Frontenac."

"Monsieur de Tonty," remonstrated the subordinate, "I know him well. He was here a month. He told me he was enlisted at St. Domingo, while Monsieur de la Salle lay in a fever, to replace men who deserted. He is a pilot and his name is Teissier."

"Whatever his real name may be we had him here on the Rock before you came, and he was called Jolycœur."

"At any rate," said Du Lhut, "his being of Abbé Cavelier's company argues that he hath done La Salle no late harm."

Tonty thought about the matter while light grew in the sky, but dismissed it when the priest of Fort St. Louis summoned his great family to matins. On such pleasant mornings they were chanted in the open air.

The sun rose, drawing filaments from the mass of vapor like a spinner, and every shred disappeared while the eye watched it. Preparations went forward for breakfast, while children's and birds' voices already chirped above and below the steep ascent.

One urchin brought Tonty a paper, saying it was Monsieur Joutel's, the young man who slept in the storehouse and was that morning gone from the fort.

"Did he tell you to give it to me?" inquired Tonty.

"Monsieur," complained the lad, "he pinned it in the cap of my large brother and left order it was to be given to you after two days. But my large brother hath this morning pinned it in my cap, and it may work me harm. Besides, I desire to amuse myself by the river, and if I lost Monsieur Joutel's paper I should get whipped."

"I commend you," laughed Tonty, as he took the packet. "You must have no secrets from your commandant."

The child leaped, relieved, toward the gate, and this heavy communication shook between the iron and the natural hand. Tonty spread it open on his right gauntlet.

He read a few moments with darkening countenance. Then the busy people on the Rock were startled by a cry of awful anguish. Tonty rushed to the centre of the esplanade, flinging the paper from him, and shouted, "Du Lhut—men of Fort St. Louis! Monsieur de la Salle has been murdered in that southern wilderness! We have had one of the assassins hiding here in our storehouse! Get out the boats!"

Men and women paused in their various business, and children, like frightened sheep, gathered closely around their mothers. The clamorous cry which disaster wrings from excitable Latins burst out in every part of the fortress. Du Lhut grasped the paper and read it while he limped after Tonty.

With up-spread arms the Italian raved across the open space, this far-reaching calamity widening like an eternally expanding circle around him. His rage at the assassins of La Salle—among whom he had himself placed a man whom he thought fit to be trusted—and his sorrow broke bounds in such sobs as men utter.

"Oh, that I might brain them with this hand! Oh, wretched people on these plains! What hope remains to us? What will become of all these families, whose resource he was, whose sole consolation! It is despair for us! Thou wert one of the greatest men of this age,—so useful to France by thy great discoveries, so strong in thy virtues, so respected, so cherished by people even the most barbarous. That such a man should be massacred by wretches, and the earth did not engulf them or the lightning strike them dead!"[24]

Tonty's blood boiled in his face.

"Why do you all stand here like rocks instead of getting out the boats? Get out the boats! They stripped my master; they left his naked body to wolves and crows on Trinity River. Get ready the canoes. I will hunt those assassins, down to the last man, through every forest on this continent!"

"You did not finish this relation,"[25] shouted Du Lhut at his ear. "Can you get revenge on dead men? The men who actually put their hands in the blood of La Salle are all dead. Those who killed not each other the Indians killed."

Tonty turned with a furious push at Du Lhut which sent him staggering backward.

"Is Jolycœur dead? I will run down this forgiving priest of a brother of Monsieur de la Salle's, and the assassin he harbored here under his protection he shall give up to justice!"

"Thou mad-blooded loyal-hearted Italian!" exclaimed Du Lhut, dragging him out of the throng and holding him against a tree, "dost thou think nobody can feel this wrong except thee? I would go with thee anywhere if it could be revenged. But hearken to me, Henri de Tonty; if you go after the Abbé it will appear that you wish to strip him of the goods he bore away."

"He brought an order from Monsieur de la Salle," retorted Tonty. "On that order I would give him the last skin in the storehouse. What I will strip him of is the wretch he carries in his forgiving bosom!"

"And you will put a scandal upon this young girl your bride, who has this sorrow also to bear. Are you determined to denounce her uncle and her brother before this fortress as unworthy to be the kinsmen of La Salle? She has now no consolation left except in you. Will you burn the wound of her sorrow with the brand of shame?"

Tonty leaned against the tree, pallor succeeding the pulsing of blood in his face. He looked at Du Lhut with piteous black eyes, like a stag brought down in full career.

"The Abbé Cavelier," Bellefontaine was whispering to one of the immigrants, "carried from this fortress above four thousand livres worth of furs, besides other goods!"

"And left mademoiselle married without fortune," muttered back the other. "He did well for himself by concealing the death of Sieur de la Salle."

Men and women looked mournfully at each other as Tonty walked across the fort and shut himself in his house. They wondered at hearing no crying within it such as a woman might utter upon the first shock of her grief. With La Salle's own instinct Barbe locked herself within her room. It was not known to the people of Fort St. Louis, it was not known even to Tonty, how she lay on the floor with her teeth set and faced this fact.

Tonty sat in his door overlooking the cliff all day.

Clouds sailed over the Rock. The lingering robins quarrelled with crows. That glittering pinnacled cliff across the ravine shone like white castle turrets. Smoke went up from the lodges on the plains as it had done during the six months La Salle's bones were bleaching on Trinity River; but now a whisper like the whisper of wind in September corn-leaves was rushing from lodge to lodge. Tonty heard tribe after tribe take up the lament for the dead.

Not only was it a lament for La Salle; but it was also for their own homes. He and Tonty had brought them back from exile, had banded them for strength and helped them ward off the Iroquois. His unstinted success meant their greatest prosperity. The undespairing Norman's death foreshadowed theirs, with all that silence and desolation which must fall on the Rock of St. Louis before another civilization possessed it.

Night came, and the leaves sifted down in its light breeze as if only half inclined to their descent. The children had been quieted all day. To them the revelry of the night before seemed a far remote occasion, so instantly are joy and trouble set asunder.

The rich valley of the Illinois grew dimmer and dimmer under the starlight. Tonty could no longer see the river's brown surface, but he could distinguish the little trail of foam down its centre churned by rapids above. Twisted pines, which had tangled their roots in everlasting rock, hung below him, children of the air. Some man of the garrison approached the windlass and let down the bucket with creak and rattle. He waited with the ear of custom for its clanking cry as it plunged, its gurgle and struggle in the water, and the many splashes with which it ascended.

His face showed as a pale spot in the dusk when he rose from the doorstep and came into the room to light a candle. Barbe must be brought out from her silent ordeal and comforted and fed.

Tonty set his lighted candle on a table and considered how he should approach her door. The furniture of the room had been hastily carried in that morning from its uses in the fête. The apartment was a rude frontier drawing-room, having furs, deer antlers, and shining canoe paddles for its ornaments.

While Tonty hesitated, the door on the fortress side opened, and La Salle stepped into the room.

Tonty's voice died in his throat. The joy and terror of this sight held him without power to move.

It was La Salle; a mere shred of his former person, girt like some skeleton apostle with a buffalo hide which left his arm bones naked as well as his journey roughened feet. Beard had started through his pallid skin, and this and his wild hair the wilderness had dressed with dead leaves. A piece of buffalo leather banded his forehead like a coarse crown, yet blood had escaped its pressure, for a dried track showed darkly down the side of his neck. Tonty gave no thought to the manitou of a waterfall from whose shrine La Salle had probably stripped that Indian offering of a buffalo robe. It did not seem to him incredible that Robert Cavelier should survive what other men called a death wound, and naked, bleeding, and starving, should make his way for six months through jungles of forest, to his friend.

Hoarse and strong from the depths of his breast Tonty brought out the cry,—

"O my master, my master!"

"Tonty," spoke La Salle, standing still, with the rapture of achievement in his eyes, "I have found the lost river!"

He moved across the room and went out of the cliff door. His gaunt limbs and shaggy robe were seen one instant against the palisades, as if his eye were passing that starlit valley in review, the picture in miniature of the great west. He was gone while Tonty looked at him.

The whisper of water at the base of the rock, and of the sea's sweet song in pines, took the place of the voice which had spoken.

A lad began to carol within the fortress, but hushed himself with sudden remembrance. That brooding body of darkness, which so overlies us all that its daily removal by sunlight is a continued miracle, pressed around this silent room resisted only by one feeble candle. And Tonty stood motionless in the room, blanched and exalted by what he had seen.

Barbe's opening her chamber door startled him and set in motion the arrested machinery of life.

"What has been here, monsieur?" she asked under her breath.

Tonty, without replying, moved to receive her, crushing under his foot a beech-nut which one of the children of the fortress had dropped upon the floor. Barbe's arms girded his great chest.

"Oh, monsieur," she said with a sob, "I thought I heard a voice in this room, and I know I would myself break through death to come back to you!"

VI.
TO-DAY.

It is recorded that the Abbé Cavelier and his party arrived safely in France, and that he then concealed the death of La Salle for awhile that he might get possession of property which would have been seized by La Salle's creditors. He died "rich and very old" says the historian,[26] though he was unsuccessful in a petition which he made with his nephew to the king, to have all the explorer's seigniorial propriety in America put in his possession. Like Father Hennepin—who returned to France and wrote his entertaining book to prove himself a greater man than La Salle—the Abbé Cavelier was skilful in turning loss to profit.

It is also recorded that Henri de Tonty, at his own expense, made a long search with men, canoes, and provisions, for La Salle's Texan colony—left by the king to perish at the hands of Indians; that he was deserted by every follower except his Indian and one Frenchman, and nearly died in swamps and canebrakes before he again reached the fort on the Illinois.

To-day you may climb the Rock of St. Louis,—called now Starved Rock from the last stand which the Illinois made as a tribe on that fortress, a hundred years ago, when the Iroquois surrounded and starved them,—and you may look over the valley from which Tonty heard the death lament arise.

A later civilization has cleared it of Indian lodges and set it with villages and homesteads. A low ridge of the old earthwork yet remains on the east verge. Behind the Rock, slopes of milk-white sand still stretch toward a shallow ravine. Beyond that stands a farmhouse full of the relics of French days. The iron-handed commandant of the Rock has left some hint of his strong spirit thereabouts, for even the farmer's boy will speak his name with the respect boys have for heroic men.

Crosses, beads, old iron implements, and countless remains of La Salle's time, turn up everywhere in the valley soil.

Ferns spring, lush and vivid, from the lichened lips of that great sandstone body. The stunted cedars lean over its edge still singing the music of the sea. Sunshine and shade and nearness to the sky are yet there. You see depressions in the soil like grass-healed wounds, made by the tearing out of huge trees; but local tradition tells you these are the remains of pits dug down to the rock by Frenchmen searching for Tonty's money. At the same time, local tradition is positive that Tonty came back, poor, to the Rock to die, in 1718.

Death had stripped him of every tie. He had helped to build that city near the Mississippi's mouth which was La Salle's object, and had also helped found Mobile. The great west owes more to him than to any other man who labored to open it to the world. Yet historians say the date of his death is unknown, and tradition around the Rock says he crept up the stony path an old and broken man, helped by his Indian and a priest, died gazing from its summit, and was buried at its west side. The tribes, while they held the land, continued to cover his grave with wild roses. But men may tread over him now, for he lies lost in the earth as La Salle was lost in the wilderness of the south.

No justice ever was done to this man who gave to his friends with both hand of flesh and hand of iron, caring nothing for recompense; and whom historians, priests, tradition, savages, and his own deeds unite in praising. But as long as the friendship of man for man is beautiful, as long as the multitude with one impulse lift above themselves those men who best express the race, Henri de Tonty's memory must stand like the Rock of St. Louis.[27]

THE END.

FOOTNOTES:

[1] Frontenac was the only man the Iroquois would ever allow to call himself their father. All other governors, English or French, were simply brothers.

[2] "Henri de Tonty, surnommé Main-de-fer." Notes Sur Nouvelle France.

[3] The romancer here differs from the historian, who says Father Hennepin met La Salle at Quebec.

[4] "This name was in Huron and Iroquois the translation of the name of M. de Montmagny (Mons maguns, great mountain). The savages continued calling the successors of Governor Montmagny by the same name, and even to the French king they applied the title 'Great Ononthio.'" Translated from note on page 138, tome 1, Garneau's Histoire du Canada.

[5] The asceticism here attributed to Mademoiselle Jeanne le Ber was really practised by the wife of an early colonial noble. See Parkman's Old Régime, p. 355.

[6] Several historians identify Jolycœur with the noted coureur de bois and writer, Nicolas Perrot. But considering the deed he attempted, the romancer has seen fit to portray him as a very different person.

[7] Historians return Father Hennepin to France in 1681.

[8] Parkman.

[9] Manuscript relating to early history of Canada.

[10] In reality this was Father Membré's adventure.

[11] "He (La Salle) gave us a piece of ground 15 arpents in front by 20 deep, the donation being accepted by Monsieur de Frontenac, syndic of our mission." From Le Clerc.

[12] Relation of Henri de Tonty (cited in Margry, I). "Comme cette rivière se divise en trois chenaux, M. de la Salle fut descouvrér celuy de la droite, je fus à celuy du mileu et le Sieur d'Autray à celuy de la gauche."

[13] Abridged from Francis Parkman's version of La Salle's proclamation. The Procès Verbal is a long document.

[14] Sanomp was suggested to the romancer by La Salle's faithful Shawanoe follower, Nika, and an Indian friend and brother in "Pontiac."

[15] Guardian Manitou. See Introduction to "Jesuits in North America."

[16] The romancer differs from the historian—Charlevoix, tome 2—who records that Catharine Tegahkouita died in 1678.

[17] Joutel. English Translation "from the edition just published at Paris, 1714 A. D."

[18] "Le Rocher," this natural fortress was commonly called by the French. See Charlevoix.

[19] "On his return he brought back with him the families of a number of French immigrants, soldiers, and traders. This arrival of the wives, sisters, children, and sweethearts of some of the colonists, after years of separation, was the occasion of great rejoicing."—John Moses' History of Illinois.

[20] "He was loved and feared by all," says St.-Cosme.

[21] Tonty's words in "Dernieres Decouvertes dans L'Amerique Septentrional."

[22] Parkman states its actual height to be only a hundred and twenty-five feet.

[23] "The joyous French held balls, gay suppers, and wine parties on the Rock."—Old History of Illinois.

[24] Translated from Tonty's lament over La Salle in "Dernieres Decouvertes dans L'Amerique Septentrional."

[25] Joutel's Journal gives a long and exact account of La Salle's assassination and the fate of all who were concerned in it. The murder, by the conspirators, of his nephew Moranget, his servant Saget, and his Indian hunter Nika—which preceded and led to his death—is not mentioned in this romance.

To this day it is not certainly known what became of La Salle's body. Father Anastase Douay, the Récollect priest who witnessed his death, told Joutel at the time that the conspirators stripped it and threw it in the bushes. But afterward he declared La Salle lived an hour, and he himself confessed the dying man, buried him when dead, and planted a cross on his grave. So excellent a historian as Garneau gives credit to this story.

In reality the Abbé Cavelier and his party treated Tonty with greater cruelty than the romancer describes. They lived over winter on his hospitality, departed loaded with his favors, and told him not a word of the tragedy.

Joutel's account of it, much condensed from the old English translation, reads thus:—

> "The conspirators hearing the shot (fired by La Salle to attract their attention) concluded it was Monsieur de la Sale who was come to seek them. They made ready their

arms and Duhaut passed the river with Larcheveque. The first of them spying Monsieur de la Sale at a Distance, as he was coming towards them, advanced and hid himself among the high weeds, to wait his passing by, so that Monsieur de la Sale suspected nothing, and having not so much as charged his Piece again, saw the aforesaid Larcheveque at a good distance from him, and immediately asked for his nephew Moranget, to which Larcheveque answered, That he was along the river. At the same time the Traitor Duhaut fired his Piece and shot Monsieur de la Sale thro' the head, so that he dropped down dead on the Spot, without speaking one word.

"Father Anastase, who was then by his side, stood stock still in a Fright, expecting the same fate,... but the murderer Duhaut put him out of that Dread, bidding him not to fear, for no hurt was intended him; that it was Dispair that had prevailed with them to do what he saw....

"The shot which had killed Monsieur de la Sale was a signal ... for the assassins to draw near. They all repaired to the place where the wretched corpse lay, which they barbarously stripped to the shirt, and vented their malice in opprobrious language. The surgeon Liotot said several times in scorn and derision, There thou liest, Great Bassa, there thou liest. In conclusion they dragged it naked among the bushes and left it exposed to the ravenous wild Beasts.

"When they came to our camp ... Monsieur Cavelier the priest could not forbear telling them that if they would do the same by him he would forgive them his" (La Salle's) "murder.... They answered they had Nothing to say to him.

... "We were all obliged to stifle our Resentment that it might not appear, for our Lives depended upon it.... We dissembled so well that they were not suspicious of us, and that Temptation we were under of making them away in revenge for those they had murdered, would have easily prevailed and been put in execution, had not Monsieur Cavelier, the Priest, always positively opposed it, alleging that we ought to leave vengeance to God."

The Récollet priest, who had seen La Salle's death, answered no questions at Fort St. Louis. Teissier, one of the conspirators, had obtained the Abbé's pardon. The others could truly say La Salle was well when they last saw him.

[26] Parkman.

[27] "In 1690 the proprietorship of Fort St. Louis was granted to Tonty jointly with La Forest.... In 1702 the governor of Canada, claiming that the charter of the fort had been violated, decided to discontinue it. Although thus officially abandoned it seems to have been occupied as a trading post until 1718. Deprived of his command and property, Tonty engaged with Le Moyne d'Iberville in various successful expeditions."—John Moses' History of Illinois.

Milton Keynes UK
Ingram Content Group UK Ltd.
UKHW030909151124
451262UK00006B/859